MEANWHILE
BACK AT THE RANCH

A NOVEL

KINKY FRIEDMAN

SIMON & SCHUSTER
New York   London   Toronto   Sydney   Singapore

SIMON & SCHUSTER
Rockefeller Center
1230 Avenue of the Americas
New York, NY 10020

SIMON & SCHUSTER and colophon are registered trademarks
of Simon & Schuster, Inc.

For information regarding special discounts for bulk purchases,
please contact Simon & Schuster Special Sales at
1-800-456-6798 or business@simonandschuster.com

Manufactured in the United States of America

10   9   8   7   6   5   4   3   2   1

Library of Congress Cataloging-in-Publication Data

Friedman, Kinky.
Meanwhile back at the ranch / Kinky Friedman.
p. cm.
1. Private investigators—Texas—Fiction. 2. Missing children—Fiction.
3. Texas—Fiction. 4. Cats—Fiction. I. Title.

PS3556.R527 M43 2002
813' .54—dc21   2002070698

ISBN 978-1-4165-7802-4
ISBN   1-4165-7802-1

ACKNOWLEDGMENTS

I'd like to thank my longtime editor Chuck Adams. Many people don't realize that Chuck was the man who first discovered Nancy Drew. Unfortunately, he then discovered Chivas Regal.

I'd also like to thank my agent, David Vigliano, for cutting short his yoga seminar in Utah to preside over my flourishing, at times rather quixotic, literary career.

Many lay readers tend to confuse the work of the agent with the work of the editor. An agent's role is to be a taker in a giver's body. An editor's job is to take something great and make it good. Agents and editors can be mean little boogers but we can't do without 'em.

I'd be quite remiss if I didn't also thank my cat, Lady, who is twenty years old and sat on my lap as I typed this manuscript, her head perfectly equidistant between my hands, her whiskers barely grazing each of them. On a number of occasions Lady would walk across the keyboard and do a little typing herself. Her contributions sailed by the usually anal-retentive production editor, Ted Landry. This could, of course, be chalked off to similarity of style. Lady and I have grown quite close over the years.

I'd also like to thank Steve Rambam, technical consultant; Cheryl Weinstein, a great friend at Simon & Schuster; and Max Swafford, Maxie, Maxie, Spiritual Taxi, for all of their efforts on my behalf. And then I'd like to thank Jesus, the world's first great Jewish troublemaker. I'm glad to hear your book's doing well, Jesus. By the way, who's your agent?

Okay, these acknowledgments are starting to cut into my cocktail hour. I've got to close now anyway. Things have been a little rough for me lately. I lost my wife last month.

In a poker game.

Kinky Friedman
Men's Homosexual Garden Club
Medina, Texas

For Cousin Nancy and Tony:
Two good people working in the world

"Where is man without the beasts? If all the beasts were gone, man would die from a great loneliness of spirit."
—*Chief Seattle*

PART ONE

NEW YORK

ONE

Like a jaded, Jewish juggler in the cheap sideshow of life, one cold, gray afternoon I suddenly found myself with five balls in the air. Unfortunately, two of them were my own. Ah, but the other three! That's where the story really began. For the first time since God gave Gatorade to the Israelites, I had three potentially big cases all going for me at once. Many aspects of this investigative trinity were so daunting that I'd taken to referring to each case with a code name. Rambam, my half-Jewish, half-law-abiding P.I. pal, had provided the three investigations with their cryptic monikers. I was not wild about the three names he'd chosen, but at least they provided a handy way to converse clandestinely about these matters, thereby keeping the other Village Irregulars in total innocence.

"I'm just not sure," I said to the cat, "that Moe, Larry, and Curly are quite the correct nomenclature for matters of this import."

The cat, of course, said nothing. She contented herself with sitting precisely in the middle of the desk and looking at me with pity in her eyes. This did not surprise me. Cats, like many people, have almost no sense of humor. The last thing on the planet liable to entertain a cat would be the Three Stooges.

3

All I knew about the cases at this point was as follows: As regards to Moe, I was four steps behind a possible serial killer. As far as Larry went, I was tantalizingly close to locating a missing autistic child who only said the word "shnay." As far as Curly was concerned, I can say nothing at all except that the investigation was so big it made the Giant Rat of Sumatra look like Mickey Mouse.

For a few furious hours, I manned the phones, talking tersely to Rambam, New York Police Detective Sergeant Mort Cooperman, Detective Sergeant Buddy Fox, and various other concerned parties whose identities I feel morally obligated to protect at this time. I maintain two red telephones on my desk, both attached to the same line and both placed precisely equidistant from the cat. If I'd had a million red telephones, I felt, I'd still not be on top of things. Finally, I took a break. I lit my third Cuban cigar of the day and walked over to the window to watch the garbage trucks. It's a little funny and a little sad to see the things people throw away in their lives. Some of them won't even fit into a garbage truck.

The only sound within the loft emanated from my commercial-sized espresso machine, which appeared to be dangerously close to liftoff. The hissing, steaming, gurgling tones sounded very much like "Blowin' in the Wind" being performed by a drowning kazoo player. I myself, worn to a frazzle from attempting to conduct three investigations at once, felt like a man dying of syphilis at the turn of the century. The cat, as one might expect, was invariably in a mood that ran counter to my own. She practically frolicked along the windowsill in unbridled, John Denver-like joy.

"It's almost good to be alive," I said, paraphrasing my father.

The cat did not respond. She did not believe in paraphrasing anybody. If a cat can't quote things precisely, the cat nearly always prefers to remain silent. If people pursued this same feline wisdom there'd be a lot fewer misunderstandings, a lot fewer wars, and a lot fewer people ripping off Oscar Wilde at cocktail parties.

I drew a hot, bitter espresso from the giant, gleaming dildo that took up about a third of my little kitchen and wandered back over to the window and stood with the cat, watching some more garbage trucks. There were worldfuls of garbage trucks and worldfuls of cats and worldfuls of people like me wondering where the hell everybody went. As far as a financial pleasure for the Kinkster went, my previous three cases might've just as well ridden out on one of the garbage trucks. I'd managed to cajole the Village Irregulars into infiltrating Winnie Katz's lesbian domain in the loft above and wound up wearing a red wig. I'd tackled a cell of international terrorists and was just happy to finally have the severed finger removed from the freezer compartment of my refrigerator. I'd also attempted to locate McGovern, who'd disappeared off the coast of Hawaii while researching recipes for his cookbook, *Eat, Drink, and Be Kinky.* He was eventually found with a little help from one of Stephanie DuPont's four-legged friends, an intrepid young Maltese named Baby Savannah.

Even though there'd been no payoff and the cases all had mixed results, I nonetheless took a small measure of pride in the seminal role I'd performed in my recent work. Had I not been successful, I thought, the world might've been overrun with lesbians and terrorists and McGovern might've been still wandering around lost in a fog somewhere. There are those, of course, who might point out that that's a fairly accurate description of how things are these days anyway.

My past triumphs and defeats, however, were all smoke now, I thought, as I glanced at my dusty reflection in the windowpane. The puppethead, which currently resided atop the mantel of the fireplace, had watched it all go down and now seemed to be smiling at me with a little wooden smile on its face. It was, I noticed, almost precisely the same little wooden smile I was currently wearing myself. Like father, like son. It pays to have a sense of humor in this life. If you don't, Allah knows what will happen.

I was puffing rather pridefully on my cigar, thinking of how challenging and potentially profitable my three new cases might be, when the phones rang. It could well be a call regarding Moe, Larry, or Curly which would, no doubt, send me into another fugue of feverish activity. I rapidly finished feeding the cat a can of Flaked Tuna with Egg Bits in Sauce, goose-stepped over to the desk, and picked up the blower on the left.

"Start talkin'," I said.

"Kinky!" said a highly excited, out-of-breath-sounding female voice. "It's Cousin Nancy from Utopia!"

I puffed stoically on the cigar, settling back in my chair for what could be a long winter. I blew a patient plume of blue smoke upward toward Winnie Katz's lesbian dance class.

"Come in, Berlin," I said.

T W O

o one in the history of the Western world has ever told
Cousin Nancy that he was too busy to talk to her and
lived not to talk to her. She is a very dedicated, ruthlessly
persistent person who is not really my cousin, does really
live in Utopia, and always gets what she wants. What she
wanted at the moment, apparently, was to talk to me.

"I hope I haven't called at a bad time," she said.

"What would make you think that?" I said. I puffed patiently
on the cigar, leaned further back in my chair, and waited for a
wave of words to make a path for one Red Sea Pedestrian to walk
toward freedom.

"I can call you at another time," she said, with a tone of disappointment bordering on brokenheartedness in her voice.

"No. Go on, Nancy," I said, starting to feel badly about my
brusque behavior. "Is everything all right in Utopia?"

"That's what I was calling about," she said, like a child who'd
been suddenly vindicated. "Some things are going on around
here that're really *upsetting* me."

Some things were going on around here, I thought, that were
really upsetting *me*. One of them was listening to Nancy not getting to the point while the three black helicopters that were Moe,

Larry, and Curly were whirring around my head. But Nancy already had me in her tenacious grip, and to cradle the blower now would be unthinkable. Besides, she had a heart of gold. She wasn't my cousin, but she was my spiritual sister. And Utopia, if you didn't already know, was Utopia, Texas. Several years back, in what seemed like another lifetime, Nancy Parker and I had founded the Utopia Animal Rescue Ranch. Nancy was now the director of the ranch and her husband, Tony Simons, was the ranch manager. My role has been occasionally described as "Gandhi-like figure."

"Tell me what's upsetting you," I said.

"Animals seem to be disappearing in this area," she said.

I had a fond, lingering image of Cousin Nancy as a Robin Hood in overalls, along with my sister Marcie and several friends, the first time they swept into the pound in Kerrville liberating seven of the most soulful-looking dogs I'd ever seen in my life. They brought "the Magnificent Seven," as Nancy called them, to Dr. William Hoegemeyer's Animal Clinic for shots and neutering before taking them to the Rescue Ranch. Then Nancy and Marcie, feeling remorseful about leaving the rest of the dogs back at the pound, made a return trip and rescued the seventeen remaining animals literally from death's door. That was probably the day the Rescue Ranch truly came into being. It now was the residence of over seventy dogs, hundreds already having been adopted into caring homes.

"Did you hear me?" Nancy asked. "Animals are *disappearing!*"

"What kind of animals?"

"Two of our neighbor's goats."

"Maybe they were taken by local Hispanic craftsmen."

"Three dogs have disappeared in town."

"Has a Vietnamese family moved in lately?"

"Oh, I know it's supposed to be happening in lots of places, but it's never happened around here before. Have you ever listened late at night on the radio to Art Bell?"

"The crazy guy who lives in a trailer?"

"There's people who say you're a crazy guy who lives in a trailer."

"Only in the summertime. And I've got nothing against people who live in trailers. Jim Rockford lived in a trailer. The king of the gypsies lived in a trailer. Hold the weddin'! I remember hearing Art Bell's show a few times. He's always yapping about UFOs and satanic cults—"

"That's him. People here follow him religiously."

"Well, maybe the animals got bored listening to Art Bell too much and they wandered away—"

"This is a small town, Kinky, and everybody knows everybody. *Something* is going on, I'm telling you—"

"Nancy, we can't save every animal on the planet. All we can do is try to open the gates of heaven a little bit wider—"

"I know. You tell me that every time I get upset."

"That's because those gates are hard to open."

"We do have some good news," Nancy said, in that maddening way some women have of turning their emotions on a dime. "Domino got adopted!"

I remembered Domino well. He was a beautiful black and white spaniel who'd been brought in one night by a drunken asshole from San Marcos who told Nancy he was going to shoot him if we didn't take him. The man said the dog's name was Cujo and that he hated all men. Nancy named him Domino and soon discovered that the dog loved everybody—man, woman, child, dog, and cat. The only person on the planet that Domino didn't like, apparently for very good reason, was the drunken asshole from San Marcos.

"Hurray for Domino!" I said.

"There's also a woman from Austin named Nancy Niland who's pledged the money to dig a well for us here at the Rescue Ranch."

"That'll cost a lot. Why is she doing it?"

"Maybe she wants to open the gates of heaven a little bit wider," said Nancy.

The Rescue Ranch, I reflected, survived on the kindness of strangers. That, and the love and hard work of Nancy and Tony.

"That's great," I said. "Look, Nancy, I've really got to bug out for the dugout now. I've got three big cases—"

"One more thing," said Nancy. "I've got a good hunting story for you. Happened nearby in Vanderpool just last week."

"Really?" I said enthusiastically. "A hunting accident?"

"You can decide for yourself. Three hunters went deer hunting and they separated and in the evening only two came back."

"I like this story already."

"They searched that night and the next day and couldn't find the guy. Big guy in his forties. Took three guns with him. They finally found him right next to this big buck he'd killed. Apparently, he'd got so excited he had a heart attack and died and they found him in a state of rigor mortis in the sitting position."

"I *love* this story."

"You haven't heard the best part. Tony and I were sitting in the Lost Maples Cafe here in Utopia last week when they brought the guy right into the place, said they were looking for the justice of the peace. We're sitting there eating chicken fried steaks and they carry him right in the door dead as a doornail all dressed up in camouflage and still in the sitting position!"

"You're making this up."

"I swear to God. Talk about losin' your appetite!"

Cousin Nancy insisted upon putting Tony on the line to verify the story. After they'd hung up I felt better than I'd felt in a long time. There's nothing like a hunting accident to brighten up an otherwise gray afternoon.

"You see," I said to the cat. "God punished the hunter for killing the buck."

The cat, of course, said nothing. This was not terribly surprising either because the cat was sound asleep. She was dreaming, very possibly, of stalking the elusive wildebeest, perhaps on some great verdant plain in darkest Africa. Like most cats and most people she failed to see the humor, the irony, and the justice in hunting accidents.

"'mon, tell me, Kinkstah!" said Ratso the next day, between several almost feral attempts to suck the flesh off of a large fish head. "What new case are you working on?"

"I'm not working on any new case, Ratso," I said somewhat irritably. "I'm just trying not to hang myself from a shower rod."

We were sitting at a small table at Big Wong's right by the stairs that lead down to the dumper. Ratso had wanted to go to a new place just across Canal Street called Wing Wong's where he contended that most of Big Wong's cooks and waiters had been relocated. I hadn't noticed any significant deterioration in the food or service, however. Just the steady deterioration of everything else in the world. Another good reason to keep the Village Irregulars in innocence of my current caseload.

"Kinkstah!" Ratso continued relentlessly. "I can tell by your distracted demeanor and your shifty eyes, Kinkstah. You've got a big case and you're not sharing it with your favorite Watson."

"First of all," I said, "my eyes always look like Richard Nixon's. I was born that way—"

"No one was born that way."

"Okay, so life made me that way. Life and watching you suck on that fish head."

"I'm trying to get the cheeks. The Chinese consider fish cheeks to be a great delicacy."

"They also wrap women's feet."

"Seriously, Kinkstah. I can see the wheels turning. I *know* you've got something on your mind. What's the new case about? I hope it's got nothing to do with Winnie Katz and her lesbian dance class."

"It's not my fault that you kept attending that stupid aerobics class for more than six months after we wrapped up the investigation."

"I know, but the way that whole legion of lesbians turned on me when that vicious dyke Winnie unceremoniously dumped me from the class was enough to emasculate even the strongest male ego."

"I guess it's too late to wrap their feet."

"I was lucky I didn't have to wrap my scrotum."

Yet the affair of the lesbian dance class had not only provided me with new insights into what went on in that Sapphic retreat in the loft above me, but also had allowed me to assess who among my friends possessed the loyalty, talent, and ingenuity to become my perfect Dr. Watson. As I looked across the table at Ratso, still sucking noisily on the fish head, I realized with some finality that perfection in human beings is a quality we are destined to always seek and never attain.

"So what's the new fucking case?" said Ratso. Once again I was taken with his innate ability to send a metaphysical chain of rather lofty thought processes directly into the toilet.

"There *is* no new case, Ratso," I said. "There is, however, one small matter that has my curiosity mildly piqued."

"And what would that be, Sherlock?"

"That would be the singular occurrence of you ordering fish-head soup, my dear Ratso. My observational powers inform me that this puissant dish is not on the menu."

"Of course not, Sherlock," said Ratso, with no small measure of pride. "You've got to know somebody."

"Ah, Watson! How very like you to be in such intimate contact with the living street! Yet I wonder if it's occurred to you that 'knowing somebody' can have application not only to ordering fish-head soup but to this very life itself. If you don't truly 'know somebody' you can be in for a very empty, lonely meal. And further, Watson, to paraphrase our friend Oscar Wilde, 'The human soul is unknowable.' "

"Maybe that's why it's not on the menu."

"Humorous, Watson! Highly humorous, if not so very tragic for the condition of man in this hard and hopeless world! And, pray tell, why are fish-head soup and the human soul *not* on the menu?"

"Old menus?"

"Hardly."

"*New* menus?"

"Hardly."

"Then what's the answer to the riddle, Sherlock? Why aren't fish-head soup or the human soul on the menu?"

"Because neither," I said, "appears to be very much in demand."

FOUR

"Why didn't you just say 'Can I have the car, Dad?' " said Rambam, as he reclined comfortably in the backseat.

"Because I need you with me," I said. "I don't know that much about stakeouts."

"What's to know?" said Rambam. "You've got coffee and donuts and you stay up all night listening to Dr. Ruth."

"Has to be Dr. Ruth?"

"Has to be Dr. Ruth. She was once a Jewish terrorist, you know. Fought in the *Irqun* alongside Menachem Begin. You use a windup radio, of course. Don't want to keep the motor running or run down the battery."

I was scrunched down in the front seat of Rambam's car. He had assigned the seating arrangements; I'd provided the address of the suspect. It was half past Cinderella time. We were parked on a street somewhere in the narrow, soulless bosom of Long Island. The night was as dark as I suspected Rambam's mood would be if he'd known what a long shot the whole exercise probably was.

"There's other stuff you need, of course," Rambam continued, pulling items out of a military duffel bag. "Flashlights with red lenses to avoid using the interior lights. Did I mention the windup radio? Empty milk carton, or, as I usually prefer, empty instant coffee bottle."

"Why do you need that?"

"In case you have to go to the little private investigator's room, you idiot. On a stakeout you can't very well walk outside and urinate on somebody's lawn jockey. And I have trouble fitting my dick into an empty milk carton. A needle-dick like yourself might prefer a milk carton. I lean toward the instant coffee bottle."

"Lean toward it carefully," I said.

There was a dry chuckle from the back of the car. I scanned the dark, cookie-cutter houses up the street. The town looked like it was dead before the virus hit.

"I take it this is part of Operation Moe," said Rambam. "But why exactly are we here on this stakeout?"

"I have reason to believe," I said, "that inside that unassuming suburban house on Long Island lives a possible serial killer."

"All serial killers live inside unassuming suburban houses on Long Island," said Rambam. "How do you know it's the right guy and the right house?"

"Call it a hunchback of Notre Dame," I said.

"That's the kind of answer that can get your bell rung," said Rambam, as he picked up the little portable radio and began winding it with what seemed an unnecessary degree of intensity. "At least Dr. Ruth always gives you a straight answer."

I kept my eyes on the house up the street as we listened to a string of commercials and a mindless sportstalk radio show. Rambam kept turning the dial but was unable to find his favorite Jewish terrorist.

"Where the fuck is Dr. Ruth?" he said in great exasperation.

"She's about as hard to locate as our suspect," I said.

"Do you have any concrete evidence that proves this guy's a serial killer?"

"No. But our presence here is the result of a rather convoluted chain of deductive reasoning. I do have my methods."

This, apparently, was not the answer Rambam was looking for. He laughed darkly in the back of the car.

"Then you don't refer to him as a suspect," he said. "You refer to him as a target."

"Well, whatever the hell you want to call him, he seems to be staying at home."

"Like we should've done. Forget Moe for a minute. What about Larry? That's a missing person's case, you say?"

"That's correct."

"Who's missing? Laurel and Hardy?"

"An eleven-year-old boy named Dylan."

"Every fucking kid is named Dylan these days. Anything else?"

"Yeah. The kid's autistic. Wandered off a playground."

"Anything else?"

"Yeah. But you won't believe it."

"Try me."

"The kid only speaks one word."

"Which is?"

"Shnay."

"*Shnay?*"

"That's right. Shnay."

The back of the car was silent. The street itself seemed strangely silent. The frenetic crazy fucking New York world seemed suddenly, strangely silent. Very much, I thought, like the sounds inside the mind of an autistic child.

From the back of the car came an extremely unsettling noise.

From all appearances it was either Rambam laughing or Rambam choking to death on a donut. If it was the former, he was being alarmingly insensitive to the psychological needs of an autistic child. If it was the latter, it would be rather inconvenient for me because I'd never find the way back to Manhattan by myself. Given the increasingly insular proclivities of modern life, of course, it was within the realm of human possibility, no doubt, for me to remain on this stakeout for the rest of my life. There'd be coffee and donuts, an empty instant coffee bottle to lean toward, and I'd be avoiding marriage, divorce, funerals, social disappointments, the flu, housekeeping, nuisance phone calls, deadbeat friends, children who become hatchet murderers or homosexuals, children who become shrinks or lawyers or MBAs, children in general, adults in particular, the rush hour, taxes, car pools, condo meetings, candiru fish darting up your penis in the Amazon Basin, cancer, crabs, corns, cocaine, conference calls, crepuscular tendencies, the "Dollars and Sense" portion of CNN *Headline News*, all the rest of television as well, all radio—

"Where the *fuck* is Dr. *Ruth?*" ejaculated Rambam from the posterior regions of the vehicle, interrupting my reverie.

Almost all radio, I thought.

"Look," said Rambam, "since you don't have hard evidence, this could be the wrong house or the wrong guy. We could even have the wrong serial killer. You stay here and man the stakeout—"

"Hold the weddin'," I said, in mild alarm. "Where the hell are you going?"

"Just out on a little recon," said Rambam, an evil leer materializing in the red glow of his flashlight. "It's the fifth house on the right, you say? I'll check out the back entrance and a few of the less obvious windows. I didn't take Peeping Tom High School Equivalency for nothing."

Rambam slipped out of the car and I slipped further down in

the front seat from which vantage point I poured another cup of coffee and took another donut out of the bag. There was, no doubt, something to be said for hard evidence, police procedure, criminal profiling, painstaking routine investigative methods. But that had never been the way I'd approached a case in my fairly brief, very lucky life as a middle-aged, Jewish, amateur private investigator.

I believed in Miss Marple. I believed in Sherlock Holmes. I believed that dogs and cats knew secret truths that man, woman, or child would never learn. Maybe child, but by that time it would be too late. I believed that blood will tell. That we're all creatures of narrow habit. That studying human nature could be more enlightening than studying a case file. I believed that in order to effectively determine guilt or innocence, juries should be impaneled entirely from a population of prostitutes, bartenders, and bellmen from sleazy hotels. I believed that cowboy logic, female intuition, native sensitivity, and a perverse mind all counted for more than what some Jehovah's bystander said he saw. I believed that clicking your heels together three times might get you home or it might just mean you're a Nazi.

The fact that I believed all this horseshit was only mildly alarming to me. I lit a cigar and watched a cat cross the street. I thought of the cat back in the loft on Vandam Street. I seriously doubted if the cat was thinking of me. They never do. Or maybe they always do. Then out of nowhere another cat crossed a corner of my mind.

It was in the early morning about three and a half years ago in the Texas summertime. I was driving the kids' laundry from Echo Hill, my family's summer camp for children, into the town of Kerrville sixteen miles away. I was driving the old dusty gray pickup known to the counselors as the Gray Ghost, and I was not alone. My assistant that morning was Mr. Magoo, a black, high-eared dog that my friend Suzie had found on the porch of the Kerrville pound with his eyes still closed. Magoo was only about four inches long when Suzie saved him and bottle-fed him, but ultimately could not save herself and had to go to the people pound, but that's another story.

Magoo spotted it first. A small orange object in the middle of the road that brought the Gray Ghost to an abrupt stop just about the time the sun came up over the mountain. I got out and saw a tiny kitten, no bigger than Magoo had been as he lay on the porch of the pound. The little creature was bleeding very badly and one of its front legs had apparently been broken. I felt it was dying, and as Magoo gently nosed the kitten on the back seat, I set my ears back and gunned the Gray Ghost over to Dr. Hoegemeyer's clinic. I gave them the pathetic little animal and told them to try to save it, whatever it took. The vet who received the kitten told me it'd been shot in the leg. "Another great white hunter," I said.

The kitten's front leg was amputated; they gave him two transfusions and stitched him up with over two hundred stitches. I went over one day with McGovern, who was down visiting the ranch from New York, and we took the frail little thing out of a cage next to a large bulldog and brought him home. McGovern gave the little kitten his medicine and nursed him like a large Irish mother hen. We did not think the kitten would live, but he did. We named him Lucky.

Lucky now lives with Cousin Nancy. He is large and handsome and enjoys good relations with Nancy and Tony and the ten dogs he shares their trailer with. With only his one front paw he's already killed a rattlesnake and more mice than Cousin Nancy cares to think about. Cousin Nancy does not like Lucky to kill mice. She likes mice, too.

Maybe that was when the Rescue Ranch started, I thought. The moment Mr. Magoo and I laid eyes on Lucky. Or maybe it was when old Abbie, the much persecuted, retired hunting dog, went over to end her days in peace at Cousin Nancy's. Abbie was named after Abbie Hoffman who also ran away and hid underground at the ranch—

My thoughts had strayed rather far from the target, I suddenly realized. Stakeouts, it would seem, provided good opportunities sometimes to think of things that you really cared about. I could now see Rambam with a rueful smile on his face coming back to the car in anything but a furtive-like manner. Instead of getting in back, he slid in behind the wheel, gunned the engine, and headed the vehicle back toward Manhattan. We drove in silence for some time. Just as we emerged from the Midtown Tunnel into the city I finally asked Rambam the question that was on my mind.

"So the stakeout was a washout?" I asked.

"Shnay," he said.

FIVE

t's quite understandable," I remarked to the cat the following morning, "for Rambam to be in a snit about Moe. The stakeout was obviously premature ejaculation on my part. How was I to know there was a Brownie troop in there having a slumber party?"

The cat did not reply. She just continued to perch on the kitchen counter like an evil buzzard striving to manufacture a measure of mortification. I didn't let it get me down.

"Rambam does seem to evince a great fascination for the case known as Larry," I rambled on as I lit my first cigar of the morning with a kitchen match.

The cat gazed intently at the flame. For a moment two tiny Statue of Liberty torches burned brightly in her eyes. Then, quick as freedom, they were gone.

"Blessed is the match that kindles the flame," I said, quoting teenage freedom-fighter Hannah Senesch, who was killed by the Nazis just before Hungary was liberated by the Russians, only to be imprisoned again under the iron fist of communism. Quick as freedom.

"I don't know if Rambam is interested in Larry because it's a missing persons case, or because the autistic child only says the word 'shnay,' or because Rambam thinks *I'm* an autistic child. Of course, I haven't told him anything about Curly. I haven't told *anybody* anything about Curly."

The cat had wandered off during the early portion of my monologue and now she was busily pursuing a rather large cockroach into the rain room.

"Careful," I shouted. "It could be Franz Kafka."

The cat, of course, did not respond. The blower, however, began ringing almost on cue. I hoisted the blower on the left. The voice on the line was unpleasantly familiar, like a child molester you used to know.

"Hi, Tex," said the voice. "How's the king of crime solvers?"

It was Detective Sergeant Buddy Fox, and if I didn't know better he sounded almost solicitous.

"Busy," I said. "How's my second-favorite public servant?"

"Second favorite?" said Fox. "Who's your first?"

"Everybody else," I said.

He laughed a condescending cop laugh that went on long enough to tell me he wanted something. I hoped I had it in stock. The cupboard was pretty bare these days.

"How can I help you, Officer?" I said.

"Call me Buddy, Tex," he said. "We've been on the same side of the police barricades enough times by now."

"Okay, Buddy. How can I help you?"

"I understand you're working the Weinberg Case? Missing autistic kid?"

"Yes, uh, Buddy. That's right. Mrs. Weinberg called me three days ago. I agreed to see if I could help."

"Yeah, well, Tex, there is a way you could help. You see, we've got over two thousand man-hours into this case. The only useful thing you could do right now is to help us with your friend McGovern."

"McGovern? He already did a big piece on the disappearance of the kid two weeks ago. Why don't you contact him yourself?"

"Because we think you could help get him to do another big piece. Maybe position a picture of the kid on the front page."

"McGovern's no pushover," I said, relighting the cigar. "But I'll see what I can do."

"That's the spirit, Tex."

When I cradled the blower, I did not call McGovern. There'd been big publicity in the papers when the kid first disappeared. Now, two weeks later, if the cops still needed more big publicity it was obvious they were urinating up a rope. Instead of calling McGovern, I cajoled a strong double espresso out of the machine, puffed purposefully on my cigar, and called the Oracle of Brooklyn, Steve Rambam.

"Of *course* they haven't got shit," he said, when I informed him of good ol' Buddy's overture. "That's why they called you."

"You really know how to make a fellow feel important."

"Look. Fox said they'd put two thousand man-hours into it. That means they've dusted for fingerprints, followed all leads, talked to all witnesses, canvassed the neighborhood, knocked on every door. You've got to concentrate on what they *haven't* done."

"If I knew what it was, I'd concentrate on it."

"Okay, look. This is very likely a kidnapping. At least you'd better hope it is, because the kid can't feed himself, he can't take care of himself, he probably can't even say his own name. All he can say is 'shnay.' So if he wasn't kidnapped he's probably dead."

"So what do I do?"

"So you interview the family. You get the family to tell you something they might've been too embarrassed to tell the cops. Maybe something they just forgot to mention. Use the personal touch. People say things all the time to perfect strangers that they'd never tell the authorities. Just remember, in my experience with missing kids there's about a fifty percent chance that your clients—the family—are somehow involved in the disappearance of the victim."

"Sounds like a plan," I said doubtfully. "I'll put Larry on the front burner and let Moe and Curly circle the bowl for a while."

"Speaking of Moe, Larry, and Curly, they had a fourth brother, you know, who joined the Three Stooges later, but they still called themselves the Three Stooges."

"Tell it to the History Channel."

"His name was Shemp."

"I don't care if his name was Wayne Newton," I said. "These are stupid names for investigations and I think I'm going to drop them—"

"Big mistake," said Rambam. "They were really heavy guys. Most people today don't know this, but all four of them were Orthodox Jews from Brooklyn. Their real name was the Fine Brothers and they were all general building contractors who specialized in single-family homes."

"Tell it to Donald Trump."

"In the forties, they were as big as the Marx Brothers, also four Jewish guys from New York. It's still a very prestigious thing in Brooklyn to live in a Three Stooges–built home."

"There are places in New York where it's no doubt considered prestigious to live in a refrigerator carton. This information, while providing some fascinating spiritual trivia, is not terribly pertinent to the matter at hand—"

"I'm telling you why you should keep the names!"

"And I'm telling you that I don't understand why—if it *was* really a kidnapping—there hasn't been a ransom note."

"Look, it's been two weeks. Maybe somebody wanted a kid and went out and took one. When they find out he only says the word 'shnay,' maybe they keep him, maybe they dump him. How the hell do I know?"

"But do you think it's possible that a ransom note might still arrive?"

"By what?" said Rambam. "Pony Express?"

A
s the late afternoon shadows fell across the tired bricks and rusty fire escapes along Vandam Street I inwardly and outwardly prepared for my interview with the missing boy's parents. I put on a dusty black cowboy hat and a full-length, colorful Indian coat that my pal Robby Romero had given me years ago. The coat had been made by Native American women sewing blankets together on the res. Their methodology was not terribly dissimilar to my own piece-meal approach to the Dylan Weinberg case. I knew virtually nothing about autistic children so I decided just to treat him like an ordinary kid. Or maybe, I thought, I'd follow my dad's advice: "Treat children like adults and adults like children and you'll never go wrong." If I ever found Dylan, I promised myself, I'd treat him like an adult.

"What're you lookin' at?" I said to the cat. "I don't look like a professional crime solver?"

The cat did not respond, but it was fairly obvious to a tree that she liked the Indian coat fashion statement. Given a chance, cats will always side with Indians over cowboys. I don't know why that is.

"That's the whole point," I ejaculated. "I don't want to look like a professional anything. This way, somebody might just tell me something."

The cat's attention was starting to lag and so was mine. She wandered over to the kitchen counter and I wandered over to the desk and removed the little ceramic deerstalker cap from Sherlock's head. Then I removed three cigars from inside his head and placed them carefully in the inside pocket of my youth. Then I killed the light and ankled it over to the door. I left the cat in charge.

It was cold outside and getting dark fast. I walked down to the corner and hailed an uptown hack on Hudson.

"Where to, Chief?" said the cabbie.

"Central Park South," I said. I never especially liked to be called "Chief," but if you dress in a brightly colored Indian coat, you have to look at that possibility as an occupational hazard.

I had no prepared script for interviewing the Weinbergs. I planned to just play it as it lays and maybe I'd get lucky. On the other side of my window was block after block of noise and lights and people. I watched it all go by and didn't say a word.

The Weinbergs' building faced Central Park only a few blocks from the Carnegie Deli, which I hadn't frequented all that much since Leo Steiner had died and since they'd imposed a hefty "sharing charge" on a platter of bagels and lox. Not that I often had anyone to share with, but the idea of the extra charge struck me as kind of un-American. The phalanx of doormen at the Weinbergs' building evidently thought that I was kind of un-American, as well. They gave me a series of slow-motion fish eyes and, when one of them finally called up to the Weinbergs, he described my wardrobe, cigar, and demeanor in the kind of detail usually reserved for the police blotter.

The elevator ride to the seventh floor was relatively uneventful. The elevator man, at least, had a friendly smile. Maybe he was lonely. Just as the elevator approached seven he spoke for the first time.

"You cowboy?" he asked. "Or you Indian?"

"I'll let you know on the way down," I said.

I'd barely begun legging it up the long, luxurious hallway when I heard the voices. They weren't loud or frenzied enough to indicate violence was necessarily imminent. They were just weary and rancorous enough to indicate that the participants were man and wife. I stood in the empty hallway listening to the sounds emanating from the Weinbergs' partly opened door.

"Fuck the health insurance!" he shouted.

"Fuck you!" she screamed. "I want a divorce!"

"It'd probably be cheaper than the health insurance," he said.

"Not as cheap as your goddamn, mean-spirited, skin-flint soul," she said.

"Can I help you?" said a soft female voice directly behind me. I turned very abruptly to find a tall, gorgeous young woman with a jeweled stud embedded in the left side of her nose. She seemed quite amused by the fact that I'd almost swallowed my cigar.

"Never sneak up on a veteran," I said, recovering what poise I had in stock.

"You must be the private investigator Sylvia hired," she said, black amusement gleaming in her dark obsidian eyes. "I wouldn't pay too much attention to their little nightly melodrama. They *are* under great stress, I'm sure you know."

"Like in the *Wizard of Oz*." I said. "Pay no attention to the little man behind the curtain?"

"Something like that," she said, her eyes like pirate ships on the horizon, dark, darker, coming closer. Nothing can be learned from the eyes of a woman. Nothing and everything. And always too late.

"And who would you be?" I asked politely.

"Well, Lieutenant Columbo," she said, "I'm Julia, Victor's daughter by his first marriage. Dylan's been missing for almost two weeks now and for some reason Sylvia, my evil step-munster, thinks you can find him when nobody else has been able to."

"Smart woman," I said.

"You're an idiot, Sylvia!" shouted Victor Weinberg through the slightly open door. "Go ahead! Get a fucking divorce! Go live with your mother in New Jersey!"

"Sylvia's mother," I said.

"What about her?" said Julia.

" 'Sylvia's Mother' is a song by Shel Silverstein."

"You're going to be a lot of help," she said.

SEVEN

"When Dylan's school principal called to inform me that he was missing from the playground," said Sylvia Weinberg, "I called the police right away."

"When was that?" I asked.

"It'll be two weeks tomorrow," put in Victor emotionally. "Two weeks and they haven't come up with a damn thing."

"I'm sure they've been very thorough," I said, "as far as that goes. They've probably followed all leads, dusted for fingerprints, interviewed all witnesses, knocked on all doors, canvassed the neighborhood. That about right?"

As I recited Rambam's tired litany of routine police procedures, I watched all three Weinbergs nod like dutiful little puppets. Just thinking about the familiar nightmare of the past two weeks seemed to have an almost numbing effect upon them. Then Julia Weinberg perked up. She languorously unfolded herself from a rather low chair and stood up on her long, lovely legs.

"What can *you* do?" she asked, looking down at me like a comely graduate student studying the mating habits of a lab insect.

"Hold the weddin'," I said. "I make no promises. I will, however, tackle things with a fresh approach."

"Does anybody want some coffee?" asked Julia, drifting off toward the kitchen.

I wanted some coffee. I also wanted Julia. This gathering, of course, was not the proper forum at which to make all of my personal needs known. Mrs. Weinberg was rattling on.

"We went to the FBI," she said. "We thought for sure they would—"

"They wouldn't touch it," said Victor, wiping what could've been a tear from his eye with a handkerchief. "They said they needed evidence of kidnapping or interstate criminal activity. They wouldn't help. Dylan's gone. No one can help."

There was a sharp, rather impertinent laugh from the direction of the kitchen. Victor Weinberg touched his handkerchief to his eyes again.

"Tell me about Dylan," I said.

"Dylan is a good, sweet, intelligent little boy," said Sylvia, as if she'd repeated it often, "who is emotionally and interpersonally challenged."

Julia rolled her eyes as she brought in a tray of coffee from the kitchen. The father dabbed his eyes again with the handkerchief.

"When Dylan was very young," Sylvia continued, "we lived for a while upstate on a farm. He loved nature. He loved the animals. He was very happy there."

We all sipped coffee in silence for a few moments. Possibly they were savoring Dylan's evanescent childhood happiness before life and people and tragedy intervened. It was a rare calm moment, apparently, in the eye of their own personal hurricane. The father seemed to be coming increasingly unwrapped. The mother, at my request, got up and located a photo of Dylan for me to have. She placed it in my hand very gently, as if it were a little bird.

"He looks like a bright young boy," I said, studying the picture.

"Bright?" said the father. "He reads at high school level. He plays concertos on the piano after seeing the sheet music only one time. He can program sophisticated computers. Hell, he could probably work for NASA."

"That's all true," said Julia, standing behind her parents and catching my eye meaningfully. "He just can't seem to get from math class to science class."

It wouldn't be hard for Julia to catch anybody's eye, but, under the circumstances, there seemed to be more that she wanted to tell me. I resolved to have a little two-party focus group with her as soon as possible. The parents, as was usually the case, had a major blind spot when it came to their son. Ted Bundy's mother, I reflected, had only good things to say about her darling boy. The same was true of virtually every serial killer who ever lived. The parents claimed he was a wonderful son, always provided, of course, that he hadn't killed them first.

But this was a stretch, I realized. This kid was only eleven years old. He wasn't a serial killer. He was only a young child cursed with a little-understood affliction. It was also unfortunate for him that his parents seemed determined to try to convince the world that he was pretty much normal. Whatever that was.

"We know he's not exactly like the other kids," Sylvia was admitting. "He's very disorganized. He's on medication, of course."

"Which he doesn't have with him," said Victor, making a brief feint with the handkerchief again.

"We hoped maybe there'd be a call for ransom money," said Sylvia. "The police said they don't have the manpower to tap the line and trace the calls unless we've gotten a request from the kidnappers." She stared into space.

"Have you?" I asked.

"No," said the mother quietly. "Nothing."

"Nothing," repeated the father, now sobbing silently into his hands.

Victor's daughter gave me a sign from behind her father that the interview was over. It had been a painful experience, possibly even more painful than the earlier inquisitions by the cops, if only because hope by now had fairly well flown from its perch in the soul, leaving a great big emptiness. I stood up, put Dylan's photo in my pocket, and said a few words of encouragement to his parents. They sat there like two statues in the rain. It was a sad thing, I thought, to have someone you love out there in the world and not be able to protect him. Hell, it was sad enough just being out there in the world yourself.

Julia Weinberg walked me to the door. Then she followed me out into the hallway.

"I've got to talk to you tonight," she said.

EIGHT

J ulia Weinberg, I quickly learned, did not live with her father and her "evil step-munster." She lived in SoHo, which bordered the West Village and made the Monkey's Paw a perfectly equidistant rendezvous point. Julia, having come from a family of some social standing and moral character, had never heard of the Monkey's Paw. That, very possibly, was the reason she'd agreed to meet me there later that night.

Back at the loft I reflected darkly upon my interview with the Weinbergs. I had learned very little of substance and the experience had drained me emotionally possibly more than I'd at first realized. This was not just another case to the Weinbergs. Over the past two weeks their world had filled up with grinding, numbing grief to the point at which they looked upon me as virtually the court of last resort. I had no idea what had happened to Dylan Weinberg. I had no clue if he was alive or dead. I had no plan as to how to find him.

"Sure I found McGovern in Hawaii," I said to the cat as I paced the empty loft. "But that was dumb luck. And I had a lot of help. And I knew McGovern's habits and personality very well. And McGovern could navigate the world interpersonally. He could speak and articulate his needs and ideas and dreams. He was not a prisoner in his own body."

The cat sneezed. She was downwind from the jet trail of my cigar smoke and, I suppose, it had inadvertently drifted her way. With cats, as with people, you can never be sure whether any particular behaviors are caused by circumstances or merely attention-getting devices. The cat sneezed again and I gave her the benefit of the doubt. I stopped pacing and power-walked over to the liquor cabinet from which I withdrew a bottle of Jameson Irish Whiskey. The bottle was either half empty or half full, depending on whether you were half empty or half full of shit. I poured a stiff shot into the old bull's horn. It isn't every day you go to a rendezvous with the beautiful half sister of a missing autistic child. Besides, it's always a good idea to have a few drinks before you go to the Monkey's Paw.

The fact that I seemed to find myself attracted to Julia did not make me proud to be an American. She, as well as her parents, was obviously in a state of traumatized grief. They obviously depended on me, and I obviously didn't know what the hell I was doing except following Rambam's crappy advice about concentrating on what the cops *hadn't* done. The cops had done everything, it seemed. They'd done everything and still there were no results. I'd just have to work harder, I thought. So far, all I'd done was make a cat sneeze.

I went over to the closet and got the photo of Dylan Weinberg out of the pocket of my Indian coat and went back and poured another shot of Jameson's. I walked the Jameson's and Dylan over to my desk, set the photo of the kid up against Sherlock's head, and poured the contents of the bull's horn down my neck. The kid had Julia's eyes. What was more unsettling, they seemed to be trying to tell me something.

"C'mon, kid," I said. "Start talkin'."

The kid, of course, said nothing. The cat, likewise. Animals were disappearing around Utopia, Texas. Children were disappearing in New York. Any chance of my future happiness was disappearing with every click of the digital clock, every beat of the lesbian dance class on the ceiling above, every moment I spent alone in the world while young couples everywhere browsed for little flavored toilet soaps and talked about what movies they liked. The fact that I was happier than 95 percent of all dentists in America did little to assuage my increasingly melancholy mood. It was time to face the lonely music of a seemingly empty life.

"Hello, young lovers," I said. "Why don't you go fuck yourselves?"

"We're too busy," they said, in tiny munchken-like voices, "shopping for little flavored toilet soaps and talking about what movies we like."

I poured another shot of Jameson's into the bull's horn. It was a rather sad commentary, I reflected, that while Dylan's parents were hoping against hope that I would find their son, I was already halfway hoping that I could hose their daughter. Sad, really. To be meeting the desperate girl in a few hours and even for a moment thinking of it as a social encounter. If I was this hard up for a date, I thought, as I killed the shot of Jameson's, I've got more problems interpersonally than Dylan. Christ, what a name. Rambam was right. Every yuppie on the planet had a kid named Dylan these days. If Bob Dylan was just starting out now he'd have to find himself another Welsh poet.

How the hell did I ever get myself into these situations? People insisting upon believing in me more than I believed in myself. I took a fresh cigar from Sherlock's head and lopped the butt off it and set fire to it with a kitchen match as calmly as a kidnapper kills a child. That was the trouble with life. It's high-stakes poker, and when you lose, you stay lost.

I took a few more cigars out of Sherlock's head for the road, and I put on my Indian jacket and my cowboy hat so Julia Weinberg would recognize me in the Monkey's Paw, which wouldn't be hard since the place was about as big and about as congested as your nose. I killed the lights and headed for the door. I left the cat in charge. I left Sherlock Holmes and Dylan Weinberg staring knowingly into the hole in my soul with the sadly smiling eyes of paper and plaster saints. Just as I was walking out the door, the cat sneezed again.

"*ss-burgers?*" I shouted incredulously above the din of the bar.

"Shut up, you fool," said Julia. "It's called *Asperger's* Syndrome. It's a rather rare form of autism first diagnosed in 1948 in the literature of Hans Asperger."

We were sitting at a small table in the back room of the Monkey's Paw. Julia wore black leather pants, a black blouse, and a black scarf, all of which matched her eyes and my mood. She was drinking a Sea Breeze. I was drinking a Guinness.

"Vic and Sylvia are in no shape to talk about Dylan," said Julia. "Even before this happened they weren't very good at talking about Dylan."

"Okay," I said in a soothing voice. "Why don't you tell me about him?"

"There's a lot to tell," she said, "and there's not much vodka in this Sea Breeze."

Her eyes glittered. The diamond in her nose glittered. Since the waiter had apparently passed away, I took her glass and navigated my way into the front room hoping to make a bartender sighting. Tommy the bartender was six-four and weighed over three hundred pounds, but all of him was hidden behind an ocean of surg-

ing humanity. It required patience, persistence, and not a little ingenuity to get the dear girl's Sea Breeze strengthened, but it was
all in a night's work for a big city private investigator.

"Where'd you go for the vodka?" she said when I returned.
"Poland?"

"That's the funniest goddamn thing I've ever heard in my
life," I said, gulping about a gallon of Guinness. "Now tell me
about the kid. Tell me what Vic and Sylvia didn't want to say.
Come on. Spit it."

"The kid, as you say, is not just 'emotionally and interpersonally challenged,' as Sylvia stated. He's not merely the sweet little
boy in the photo she gave you. I don't mean to sound heartless,
but the kid is seriously fucked-up."

I thought of what my father, Uncle Tom, used to sometimes
say to the parents of certain campers at Echo Hill: "The psychological term we like to use for your child is 'a little shit.' "

"Victor told me that just a few weeks ago he woke up suddenly at three o'clock in the morning to find Dylan standing over
his bed like a zombie. Dylan had a pair of scissors in his hand and
was calmly cutting the bedsheets. It spooked Victor pretty bad."

"I can imagine."

"No, you can't. You can't imagine the pressure Daddy and
Sylvia have been under. Dylan's on psychotropic drugs—Prozac,
Ritalin, Paxil. He's drugged-out most of the time."

"I *can* imagine."

"I don't mean to sound hateful. He can't help his condition.
But it's been a lot tougher than Sylvia and Victor let on. Dylan
was making both of them crazy. He eats only brown food. If he
speaks at all it's often in an eerie, computer-like voice. He keeps a
notebook of his artwork. Hundreds and hundreds of intricately
drawn sketches of ceiling fans."

"Is there a ceiling fan in the apartment?"

"No."

"Maybe you ought to get one."

"Maybe you ought to get us another round of drinks."

As luck would have it, the ponytailed waiter was in the process of making a rare passage across the room. I was able to flag him down, order another round, and keep Julia talking about the private hell in which her family had been living. She seemed ambivalent about her half brother; at times she seemed to blame him, at other times she appeared to feel personally guilty, almost remorseful. It couldn't have been easy for any of them. I sipped the foam off another Guinness and watched the ceiling fans slowly turning in her eyes.

"It's all so horrible," she said, as the waiter flew off in a contrail of ponytail. "Dylan's out there somewhere—"

She gestured vainly toward the dark, lonely window of the Monkey's Paw. The vodka, the stress, the helplessness, the hopelessness all were making her very vulnerable. She was an interviewer's dream.

"Tell me about the inner workings of your family," I said. "I noticed some tension between Vic and Sylvia when I first came to the apartment."

"You don't miss much," she said facetiously. "As you know, I don't live there anymore. Sylvia and Daddy are always at each other. That's normal. Sylvia and I are not particularly fond of each other. That's normal. We've all tried to do the best we can to keep our lives as normal as possible under the circumstances. Dylan suffers from Asperger's Syndrome and it's not his fault. It's nobody's fault. I think Vic and Sylvia have always blamed themselves. They've felt guilty somehow, and now, particularly after the scissors incident, even afraid."

"That's understandable," I said. "It would scare the shit out of Bela Lugosi. But your dad seems to me to be especially distraught."

"Daddy and Dylan were not getting along lately, and Daddy irrationally thinks he's responsible for whatever happened. He and Dylan used to be closer. Last year, when Dylan was ten, they even worked on projects together."

"What kind of projects?"

"Well, together they built a beautiful, elaborately designed wooden airplane, and one evening Vic came home and found it smashed to pieces the size of matchsticks."

"What did Dylan have to say about it?"

"Shnay."

Julia sipped at her Sea Breeze and wiped an invisible tear from her eye. If I was ever going to have a prayer of finding this kid it was important to keep this woman's confidence. I had to keep her drinking and talking. The former appeared to be no problem. Besides, I liked a girl who would take a drink.

"What other projects did Vic and Dylan work on together?"

"Oh, well, there was the famous stock market scheme that Dylan came up with on the computer. I think he was all of nine at the time. Vic works on Wall Street, but Dylan is the natural. Dylan engineered a stock takeover of the company that was distributing *Superman III* in Nigeria—"

"Sounds like a conservative, diversified portfolio."

"He likes Superman. What can I say? Anyway, by following Dylan's stratagems—which were light years ahead of Charles Schwab, I might add—the two of them racked up a small fortune."

"So what happened?"

"Well, Vic doesn't talk about it much—"

"And Dylan doesn't talk about it."

"Funny. Vic did mention something about problems with the Nigerian government, but I think it could've just been—"

"Like what happened to the model airplane?"

"Right. Anyway, they lost everything."

It was raining outside now. We could see through the barred and latticed window how the raindrops ricocheted off the sidewalk like bullets from heaven. Because the Monkey's Paw, in more ways than one, was at a level below the street, we could see only people's feet going by outside. No faces. No bodies. Only boots and shoes walking aimlessly back and forth along the rainwept sidewalk between the avenues of destiny.

"Has there ever been anyone who you felt could really communicate with Dylan?" I said. I was working religiously on my third or fourth Guinness and Julia was keeping up with me in her Sea Breeze area. I wasn't certain at the moment whether or not anybody had ever really communicated with anybody, but there was no harm in asking.

"When the family was still living on the farm and Dylan was about four or five, a big, friendly black woman from North Carolina came to live with us. Her name was Hattie Mamajello. I don't know if that was her real name or just the one Dylan gave her."

"It's an unusual name."

"So's Richard Kinky 'Big Dick' Friedman. Anyway, I was going off to school about then, but I remember that Dylan and Hattie had a language all their own that nobody else could understand."

"Kind of like J.R.R.R.R. Tolkien?"

"Kind of," said Julia without amusement. Either her thoughts were still somewhere back at the farm or she was trying to establish eye contact with my cowboy hat.

"I recall just the two of them, Dylan and Hattie, that little boy and that big black woman, just chattering away to each other out on the front porch in the evenings. You could hardly understand a word they were saying. Now that I think about it, the word 'shnay' must've evolved from that period."

"And what, in your opinion, does the word 'shnay' mean?"

"I don't know," said Julia with some little degree of irritation. "Why don't you ask Dylan when you find him?"

"Maybe I will. Tell me more about Hattie Mamajello."

"Hattie, of course, had never had much education. I'm not even sure if she could read or write. She certainly didn't know about Asperger's Syndrome. She always contended that Dylan was different because he had 'Smilin' Mighty Jesus.' "

"Sort of like *The Shining?*"

"Kind of. It was several years before we realized what she was talking about. 'Smilin' Mighty Jesus' was just Hattie's way of saying 'spinal meningitis.' It was kind of sad really. Vic had to let her go just a few months before Dylan disappeared. He was so strapped he couldn't afford to pay her anymore."

As the rain came down harder I plied Julia Weinberg with more drinks and more questions. She talked about her "wicked step-munster" and that troubled woman's rocky relationship with her "emotionally challenged" son. According to Julia, Sylvia vaselined back and forth from excessively coddling the boy to borderline child abuse. She claimed to have seen Sylvia slap Dylan on a number of occasions.

By the time we'd left the Monkey's Paw I had a much better understanding of the inner workings of the Weinberg family, a good ongoing rapport with Julia, and a pretty fair rolling buzz for myself. As we climbed the five steps to the street we saw through the deluge possibly the only hack in New York that wasn't off duty, and I, like the southern gentleman that I was, gave it to Julia. When it rains, every cab in the city seems to go off duty. This was okay with me. I was off duty, too.

I walked across Sheridan Square to Village Cigars, getting soaked in the rain and trying to absorb what might be gleaned from the dark spiritual landscape Dylan's older half sister had painted for me. For certain psychic reasons, known perhaps only to herself, Julia almost violently believed the boy to be alive. I was not so sure. Possibly I was just old enough not to be so sure of anything.

Under an awning by Village Cigars I saw a crippled veteran from some forgotten war huddling on the sidewalk with his dog. The man's eyes were war-torn and the dog's eyes were sad and peaceful. I gave the man a twenty-dollar bill.

"God bless you, mister," he said. "What's your name?"

"Smilin' Mighty Jesus," I said.

TEN

It rained for forty days and forty nights. I holed up in the loft eating takeout food from Big Wong's, drinking Jameson Irish Whiskey punctuated with the occasional espresso to keep me from constantly walking on my knuckles, smoking cigars to remind me that life was smoke, and reading a cheap, pulp mystery novel called *The Cat Who Killed Christ*. I read at a remedial pace. Indeed, the world itself seemed to move at a remedial pace. Maybe God was on downers. Maybe it was just the rain.

From my vantage point on the davenport I could see the rain falling, ruthless and cruel like dishwater daggers, like silver millions of knives plunging gentle, oblique, silver, silently silver, into the hearts of the lovers at the end of the dream. Somewhere up the Hudson River three homeless men, Che Guevara, Hank Williams, and Adlai Stevenson, were building an ark. The chief carpenter was Father Damien of Molokai who embraced the lepers and like Jesus was a carpenter by trade. The trees he used for timber to build the ark were the only ones he could find that hadn't already been killed to make all of them Dean Koontz books. And Stephen King books. Hadn't run into Stephen King lately.

I tried futilely to glean more information about the missing autistic child who only said the word "shnay." Actually, at least according to Julia, he said a good bit more than "shnay." The only trouble was he said almost everything else in a scary, computer-like voice, which was enough to discourage most small talk, particularly when he was standing over your bed like a zombie with a pair of scissors in his hand.

In real time, the rain might've lasted for the better part of a week, during which time I visited the Weinbergs again, took copious notes in my little private investigator's notebook, took Julia to Big Wong's for lunch one day, talked to Cooperman, talked to Fox, and, at their persistent urgings, finally got around to attempting to suck, fuck, or cajole McGovern to help with the beleaguered campaign to find the kid. McGovern did not display a particularly civic-minded attitude.

"I already did a piece on this kid," said McGovern in a some-what peevish tone of voice. "Cooperman must not have shit."

"That's what Rambam said."

"He couldn't have shit if he's already coming back to me on this thing. And he doesn't even have the balls to come back to me himself. He's got to talk to *you* to talk to *me*, because he knows if *he* talks to *me*, I'll tell him to go fuck himself."

"What about a missing kid who doesn't even have face time on a milk carton yet? You going to tell him to fuck himself?"

"Thousands of kids were murdered in America during the last two or three years," said McGovern. "Most people only know the name of one of them: JonBenet Ramsey. Many more than that go missing each year. Most people only know the name of one of them: Dylan Weinberg. I've already done an in-depth, high-pro-file piece on the kid. What's your angle, anyway?"

"The Weinbergs have hired me to find their kid."

"Why didn't you just say that?" said McGovern with a loud, Irish laugh. "Then I could've just told *you* to go fuck yourself."

"Come on, pal. I need your help. Besides, it's an amazing story. Did you know that Dylan Weinberg was a stock market whiz? Did you know he can play every note ever written by Gilbert and Sullivan? Have you ever heard of Asperger's Syndrome?"

"Ass-burger's Syndrome?"

"No, you idiot! *Asperger's* Syndrome. It's a rather rare form of autism first diagnosed in the literature in 1948 by Hans Asperger."

"Okay. Okay. Let's get together and compare notes and I'll see what I can do for you. But I make no promises."

"The kid's been missing for over three weeks! Why the hell not?"

"Because I have this thing, Kinky. It's called a job. And this job has a thing. It's called my editor."

"And?"

"And I can't tell my editor to go fuck himself."

I cradled the blower and listened to the rain falling on the rusty fire escape. The rhythm of the falling rain sounded like Neil Sedaka had been bugled to Jesus and had come back outside my kitchen window to play my fire escape like a xylophone. It'd been a long time since Neil Sedaka had a big hit. Probably that was just as well. The rain would eventually stop, I reasoned. McGovern would come around and position a major story for us. The sun would come out and shine brightly on John Denver's shoulder, figuratively speaking of course, since John Denver's shoulder was currently worm bait. And, I reckoned, inevitably, I would also locate Dylan Weinberg. I felt fairly certain that all of these things would come to pass at least by the time Neil Sedaka got his next big hit.

I went out and had a big hairy steak that evening at Gallagher's with my old college roommate, Chinga Chavin. Chinga was now a vastly successful advertising magnate, but he'd once been the leader of a band called Country Porn. They'd recorded songs such as "Proud to Be an Asshole from El Paso" and, my personal favorite, "Cum Stains on My Pillow (Where Your Sweet Head Used to Be)."

"As a private investigator," I said to Chinga, once we'd had a few drinks, "I notice that you still have those little Band-Aid strips on your temples and around your fingers. From this I deduce that you remain encumbered with the same problem, self-inflicted scratching like a monkey on angel dust."

"That's essentially correct," said Chinga, "and the more successful I become the more aggravated seems the malady. If you'll remember, my shrink referred to my condition as 'a grooming mechanism gone awry.' "

"That was a brilliant diagnosis, but what's your shrink saying now?"

"He's saying, 'That'll be four hundred dollars, Mr. Chavin.' "

About halfway through the big hairy and about seventeen different kinds of fried potatoes, I employed Chinga's cell phone to check my answering machine. I was expecting calls from Julia, Rambam, Fox, and McGovern regarding the Dylan Weinberg situation. There was, however, only one message on my machine and that was a very distraught call from Utopia, Texas.

"You look upset, darling," said Chinga. "Have I said anything that may have angered you?"

"Message from Cousin Nancy," I said.

"I didn't know you had a Cousin Nancy."

"I don't."

"I see. You don't look well at all, dear. Maybe you should see my shrink."

"Not unless I can christian him down on his prices. Cousin

Nancy runs our rescue ranch for animals in Utopia, Texas. She just gave me some bad news."

"What happened?" said Chinga. "Somebody fuck a sheep?"

I stared evenly at Chinga across the table. His eyes were already glazed from four martinis and whatever else he was on. I wasn't in much better shape myself. Every misfortune that befalls an animal always takes away a little piece of your soul. Whether you know it or not.

"Animals have been mysteriously disappearing around Utopia. Now Nancy says that she's been receiving threatening phone calls."

"So have I," said Chinga.

"I doubt if your drug dealer's been calling Cousin Nancy. Anyway, the bad news is that last night Lucky, the three-legged cat, disappeared. Lucky was one of the first animals to ever live at the Rescue Ranch. He stays with Nancy, her husband, Tony, and ten dogs in a big double-wide trailer, and he never goes outside except briefly to sun himself on the front porch."

"Sounds like an inside job."

"Animals, like most people, are creatures of narrow habit. Lucky's been missing for over twenty-four hours now. He's never done this before. Frankly, I'm very worried."

"Could be foul play, Kink," said Chinga as he ordered yet another martini.

"You know," I said with some anger, "for a fucking guy who may now be a big advertising executive but who once thought of himself as a poet, your concern for all creatures great and small seems to have been seriously marginalized."

"That's not true!" shouted Chinga heatedly. "I love poetry! I love animals!"

Several waiters were in the process of clearing the table and bringing the check and they provided a nice captive audience for Chinga.

" 'A robin redbreast in a cage,' " he recited loudly, " 'Puts all Heaven in a rage.' "

The waiters stood by the table looking at Chinga quizzically. Perhaps they'd expected a bit more.

"William Blake," Chinga said to them. They nodded agreeably. One of them handed Chinga the check.

"Obviously he doesn't believe you're a poet," I said, after the waiter had left. "If he did he never would've given you the check."

"True," said Chinga, "but I do have the soul of a poet. For instance, I believe that Lucky might've paid the price for something that he was, perhaps, in one of his previous lives."

"What do you think he was?"

"An advertising executive," said Chinga.

We stumbled out of Gallagher's into the brittle New York night. It was colder. It seemed lonelier somehow. It was raining cats and dogs.

ELEVEN

By the time I got soaked, got a cab, and got back to the loft it was practically pushing Cinderella time. I shook the rain from my hat and called Cousin Nancy. It was almost eleven in Texas and Nancy and Tony usually didn't answer the phone after eight o'clock. But Nancy did answer. This was already a bad sign. As a detective, it told me that a cat who was missing three thousand miles away had not been found.

Perhaps I had forgotten how much some animals can mean to some people. Nancy sounded dazed and grief-stricken; indeed, the conversation was very similar in terms of emotional climate to my recent interview with the Weinbergs. She blamed herself, saying that she should've taken the threatening calls more seriously. She said that Lucky represented the spirit of the Rescue Ranch and that Lucky "of all people," having only three legs, didn't need this. She said she knew I was very busy in New York but, as the person who'd first found Lucky on the highway, she was praying that I could come down to Texas and find him again. This seemed highly irrational, of course, but then Nancy herself was very definitely highly agitato.

"Hold the weddin'!" I said to Nancy soothingly. "Try to relax

and let's think this through together. We don't even know for
sure that Lucky was abducted."

"Yes we *do*," Nancy insisted. "Tonight Tony found a handwrit-
ten sign on the gate. It said: YOU WON'T BE SO LUCKY NEXT TIME.
The word 'lucky' was printed in big block letters. It really fright-
ened me, Kinky, when I saw that."

"Now just take it easy, Nancy. There's nothing we can do right
now—"

"But it's *raining* outside," Nancy wailed.

"Maybe Brook Benton was right."

"What did Brook Benton say?"

" 'It's rainin' all over the world.' "

I said a few calming words to Cousin Nancy and promised I'd
call her in the morning, but she was sobbing as I cradled the
blower. I didn't mention it to her, but in missing cat cases, much
like in missing persons' cases, the first twenty-four hours are crucial. If there was no sign of the victim within those first twenty-
four hours, you could be in for a long and extremely unpleasant
movie. In this case, there'd been no sign of the victim. There had
been, however, the sign on the gate. Unfortunately, the gate was
three thousand miles away.

My cat had never met Lucky, but as we sat together in the
semi-darkness of the loft, as the smoke from my cigar twirled
upward toward the silent lesbians like the lariats of a million Lil-
liputian cowboys, as sensitive feline eyes met those of troubled
man, she knew something was wrong. She was not quite sure
what it was. Finding out, she implied, was my job.

The rain was falling harder out on Vandam Street as I killed
the lights, put on my Borneo sarong, and attempted to crash-land
on some dream island in the South Pacific. A kid was missing, a
cat was missing, and God knows what else was missing from all
of our lives, but whatever it was had been gone so long that most

of us had found something else to take its place, and forgotten that it wasn't the same. Rain always makes it easy to sleep and easy to lose things you keep. Robert Louis Stevenson was now outside in the pouring rain, playing the fire escape with a croquet mallet. He'd arrived in Hawaii in 1888, the year before Father Damien's death. He'd visited the island of Molokai mere weeks after that mortal spirit had been bugled to Jesus. He spent twelve days there teaching the girls, leprosy victims at the Bishop Home at Kalawao, how to play croquet. He said that if he hadn't left the leprosy settlement when he did, he probably would've stayed there forever. That was a pretty good description of the way I usually felt about New York.

"I know not if the interest in croquet survived my departure," Stevenson wrote, "but it was lively while I stayed; and the last time I passed there, on my way to the steamer's boat and freedom, the children crowded to the fence and hailed and summoned me with cries of welcome. I wonder how I found the heart to refuse the invitation."

The interest in croquet did not survive very long, of course. Neither did the players. Neither did Robert Louis Stevenson, who conked six years later in Samoa. Now RLS and his young leprosy patients had a new gig, apparently, on my fire escape. The croquet mallets gently pounding the rusty steel tongues of the fire escape in the night sounded beautiful beyond words and music, though most people probably would have thought it was just the rain.

In the morning I was awakened by a very unpleasant call from Ratso. The espresso machine was beckoning me, the cat was weaving figure eights around my feet waiting for breakfast, the garbage trucks were grumbling out on Vandam Street, a morning monstro-erection had turned my sarong into a small pup tent, and an abrasive, rodent-like New York voice was yapping from the blower into my left earlobe. I glanced out the window and noticed that the rain had stopped. Now if I could just get Ratso to stop.

"—and I could've been a big help on the subject of Asperger's Syndrome. You know I've got a master's in psychology from the University of Wisconsin in Madison. I would've gone ahead and got my Ph.D. but—"

"I know, Ratso," I said wearily. "You've told me before. A spider bit you on the scrotum."

"It's true! Just as I was working on my oral dissertation."

"It's too bad the spider didn't bite you on the lips so they swelled up like some giant Ubangi's and you couldn't speak to people on telephones in the morning."

"That's alarmingly racist, Kinkstah."

"Not really, Ratso. So tell me, how in the hell did you know that I might be involved with anything remotely related to Asperger's Syndrome?"

"Sorry, Kinkstah. I can't reveal my sources." As always, Ratso maddeningly pronounced the word "sources" so that it sounded like "sauces."

"Have you been talking to a large half-Irish leprechaun?"

"Can't reveal my sources, Sherlock. But did I hear it from McGovern? No. Did I hear it the other day at Big Wong's when I asked my friend the Kinkstah what new cases he was working on? No."

"That's because this is a very sensitive missing person's investigation and at the time I didn't want all the Village Irregulars to step in and fuck it up. Now, of course, it's too late."

"Maybe not, Sherlock. I do know a thing or two about Asperger's, and the Weinberg boy fits my theory perfectly. Did you know that Asperger's afflicts a highly disproportionate number of *boys?*"

"No, I didn't."

"Were you aware that Asperger's afflicts a highly disproportionate number of *firstborn* boys?"

"No, I wasn't."

"Did you know that Asperger's Syndrome afflicts a highly disproportionate number of *Jewish,* firstborn boys?"

"Who's calling, please?"

"Don't you see, Kinkstah? Hans Asperger formulated his ideas in the years immediately following the Second World War. Before that time the syndrome does not seem to have been recorded or even to exist. So here are my three theories. Since Asperger's affects so many Jewish firstborn males it could've been a misguided biblical plague which, of course, presupposes that there is a God, which makes that theory unlikely to say the least. The second theory, which makes more sense, is that Asperger's Syndrome is a condition caused by the Holocaust, which somehow is carried to its victims through the group psyche. The third theory, which I like the best, is that Hans Asperger was in reality a kraut propagandist who devised Asperger's Syndrome to cover for and explain the human deviations caused by the genetic experimentation done by the Nazis."

I watched the smoke from my first cigar of the morning drift effortlessly upward to somebody else's heaven like other smoke from long ago and far away.

"Good work, Watson," I said.

TWELVE

If you're trying to find children in trees, or dogs and cats in big green fields, or little shining pieces of happiness and love and peace in this world, you've pretty much got your work cut out for you because all these things are almost never really lost and almost never truly found. So it was that I struggled in vain through the bright and blameless morning searching for things that I knew in my heart were not there.

For some reason I put off calling Cousin Nancy for a while. I didn't want to know that Lucky was still missing in action. If, indeed, he had returned, maybe Nancy would soon be calling me in an orgasm of joy. If that happened, maybe I could concur for a few flying hours with God's pathetically optimistic observation that the world was good. God had made His remark, of course, directly after overseeing the creation of the world. Maybe it *was* good back then. Maybe it was just another case of the date on the carton having expired.

I sipped a hot, bitter espresso from my chipped Imus in the Morning coffee mug. Imus had been pretty busy lately. Too busy to return the last three phone calls from one of his oldest friends. It's never best foot forward to be so busy that you're neglectful of your oldest friends. They might just disappear someday, like

Dylan Weinberg or Lucky or your chances for future happiness. Besides, when people don't return my calls, it makes me angry, paranoid, bitter, lethargic, restless, melancholy, and often suicidal. Did I mention world-weary? It's sort of suicide lite. And I've got nothing against suicide. In fact, thoughts of suicide have gotten me through many a long and lonely night. When old friends don't return calls, it's like when the elephants are coming to our village and they are shitting on our Cheerios and we are praying to the monkey god so that our old friends will be remembering us. Anyway, fuck a bunch of old friends. Who needs old friends? Everybody does. It's getting too late to make very many more of them.

"Did you know that drunken Finnish sailors first taught the tango to prostitutes in South American whorehouses?" I said to the cat.

The cat did not respond. The cat was a right-wing Christian fundamentalist and did not enjoy hearing any portion of this information.

"Did you know," I said to the cat, "that more people die each year from getting kicked by donkeys than die in plane crashes?"

The cat really didn't give a shit about that one either. It was just as well. I was, in fact, eternally grateful to Allah that the cat had ceased her previous campaign of vindictively dumping upon every unoccupied surface of the loft. There came a time when I had to concede we would probably never command a feature in *Better Homes and Gardens*. There was a moment there when the cat turds reached to the sky in mighty castles of dry drek and I entertained the possibility that we might command a feature in *Architectural Digest*. But it was not to be.

I was on my second espresso and my second cigar of the morning when I turned my convoluted thought processes to Ratso's far-flung theories and well-kept "sauces." Ratso's theories were fascinating, if the truth be told, and, who knows, there could be something to them. I just didn't see how they were going to help me find Dylan Weinberg. The matter, however, of how Ratso knew I was handling the investigation was something I might be able to clear up right away.

"No converso with El Ratso!" said McGovern adamantly, when I called him on the subject.

"Well, he knows about it," I said.

"Most of the literate people in New York know about it," said McGovern. "They read McGovern."

"But none of them know that I've taken the case," I said. "Only you, Fox, Cooperman, and the immediate family know that."

"So ask Ratso how he found out."

"I did. He can't reveal his 'sauces.' "

"Can't reveal his *sauces?* What's he running? A chili cook-off for the C.I.A.?"

"You swear you haven't spoken to him?"

"I swear by Jesus, Joseph, and Mary. Does that about cover it?"

"Hardly," I said.

I cradled the blower wondering how in the hell Ratso had known of my involvement with the Weinbergs. It was a small mystery, but it was still a mystery. If Ratso was as clever and resourceful about finding the kid as he'd evidently been about finding out about my activities, he might yet be some help before it was all over. McGovern, apparently, was trying to be helpful as well. Before he'd rung off he'd mentioned that he was making progress with his editor about prominently positioning a new feature on the kid. The new feature, according to McGovern, would have to include my own bold intrusion into the case. I asked McGovern why, and he said "because it's the only thing new." I had no problem with people knowing I was trying to find Dylan Weinberg; the only people I hadn't wanted to know had been the Village Irregulars. Now that they all probably knew and would want to come aboard, they might just be of help despite themselves. As always, we might take something great and make it good.

Around eleven bells I called Cousin Nancy. There was still no Lucky. Nancy was still highly agitato. There was still something tugging at my heart, telling me it was time to put away my croquet mallet.

Where you go and what you do with your life is your business, not to mention who you spend it with. You want to live in a drafty loft with an antisocial cat, that's fine. You want to compromise, contort, cash in your spiritual chips, and carpool yourself to a hell that isn't even your own, that's fine, too. But sometimes in life there comes the opportunity, no matter how great or how small, to be God's own private investigator and to search for whatever it is that cannot be found. This job rarely pays very well, has no security and no pension fund, but you are your own boss and the only ceiling is the stars.

It was later that afternoon when Rambam called to deliver his weekly morality lecture. I'd forgotten over time, I suppose, that not only had he once trained to be a cop, he'd also once trained to be a rabbi. Now the mere fact that Rambam had cop and theological proclivities may not mean much. I myself once trained to be a busboy at Shoney's in Nashville, Tennessee, and I've never worked a day in my life. But the point is that Rambam had come to field a fine influence with me in the morality department. He had an extremely well-developed sense of right and wrong, which occasionally he wielded like a hammer. The laws of our country, unfortunately, did not always agree with Rambam's sense of right and wrong.

"All my little helpers," I said, quoting my father's famous rejoinder every time the Echo Hill Ranch staff screwed something up.

"Watch it," said Rambam. "Some of us are not so little. Anyway, 'shnay' means 'two' in Hebrew, and 'snow' in German. So I figure when the kid was two years old he was taken for a ride in the snow on a sled named Rosebud by an Israeli spy from the Mossad disguised as a German nanny."

"Not unless she was black and from North Carolina."

"Whatever. Okay. So let's get serious and find this kid."

"Ratso wants to help."

"I said let's get serious and find this kid."

"Ratso knows about it. McGovern knows, of course. It won't be long before Mick Brennan and Chinga Chavin are clamoring to get aboard. I feel a bit like the drunk in the elevator who says, 'Now that I have you people all together I can't remember what I wanted you for.' "

"If the drunk had been on with the Village Irregulars, he probably would've jumped down the shaft."

"The only ones who seem to be getting the shaft right now are the Weinbergs."

"So let's find the fucking kid."

"Well, that's kind of what I wanted to talk over with you. Dylan Weinberg's not the only one who's missing."

"Of course not. I've told you, thousands of kids go missing in this country every year."

I took a patient puff on my cigar. I wanted to broach the idea that had been forming in my fevered brain very carefully with Rambam. I wasn't sure how it would chime with his iron-clad code of what was right and what was wrong.

"Do you remember Lucky?" I said finally.

"The only Lucky I remember is Lucky Luciano. Crime boss

from the forties. He got the name Lucky because when they tried to rub him out he ran away weaving down the street and the hit man shot at him six times and missed every time."

"The Lucky I'm talking about is the three-legged cat Mr. Magoo and I rescued on the highway about three years ago."

"And?"

"And we took him to Cousin Nancy's and he became one of the major spiritual forces behind the founding of the Utopia Rescue Ranch."

"Very nice. And?"

"He disappeared a few days ago from Nancy's trailer. Someone left some threatening phone messages and a note out on the gate. Cousin Nancy believes Lucky was forcibly abducted. I'm inclined to agree with her."

"Very possible. And?"

"And I'm just thinking about the possibility of my going down to Texas for a few days and seeing if I can find out what happened to Lucky. I could still stay in touch with you on the Weinberg case, and some of the Village Irregulars might actually prove helpful while I was away. I was just thinking about it. I don't know what the hell I'm going to do actually. That's why I wanted to talk it over with you."

There was a long silence on the line. It was the silence of moral outrage. Through the blower I could almost hear a palpable sea change occurring in the mind and the heart of Steve Rambam. At last he spoke.

"I can't fucking believe I'm *hearing* this," he said in a voice of intense grievance and disgust as he continued to speak. "I can't fucking believe I'm hearing this from *you*. What are you? A fucking *idiot*? Which one is more important? There's a *child* missing in New York. There's a *cat* missing in Texas. I think you can probably figure it out for yourself."

PART TWO

TEXAS

THIRTEEN

s the plane dipped gracefully over the San Antonio sky-
line, many thoughts were flying through my consciousness. Of course, Rambam had a point. I could hear his
angry words of two days ago: *"Which one is more important? I think you can probably figure it out for yourself."* I could
hear Cousin Nancy's imploring tones: *"Something is going on, I'm
telling you. Can't you help us?"* I could even hear Abraham Lincoln's
words on the subject: *"I care not for a man's religion whose dog or cat
are not the better for it."* I could also hear a still, small voice res-
onating through that thing that I have often felt but never seen
called my conscience. It warned: *"Please fasten your seat belts. Our
descent could get a little bumpy."*

In this wicked, wonderful, war-torn world we each have only
so much time allotted to us, and it's important that we put our
services to some higher use than day trading or trading our status
as participants in life to that of observers of life by watching
other human idiots live, love, and die on the flat, fatuous surface
of our television screens. Personally, I've always had a better
record for locating cats than I've had for finding missing persons.
I did manage to find McGovern when he went missing in Hawaii,
but McGovern is a pretty large person and Hawaii is a pretty great

place to be searching for anyone or anything. Texas is bigger, of course. And cats are smaller.

I also had it in the back of my mind, I suppose, that by temporarily bugging out for the dugout, I might provoke Rambam, who was an expert on missing persons, to more enthusiastically leap into the fray on the Dylan Weinberg case which, as far as I could see, was moving about as fast as a garden slug on valium. Though he might bitch and moan a bit, if Rambam took the bait, the investigation might just achieve a speedier resolution. I did not say happy ending. If you want a happy ending, try Hollywood. Life's the wrong racket for you. It'll only make you cry. But there is one way you can always guarantee that you'll wake up in the morning smiling: Go to bed with a coat hanger in your mouth. Hopefully, I wouldn't have to be doing that myself. If I could spend a few days in Texas, get the Lucky situation resolved, then head back to New York quickly enough, the Weinbergs need never know that the private investigator they'd hired to find their missing son had disappeared as well.

There was not a large delegation there to meet me at the baggage claim. That was the way I wanted it. Low profile all the way. I just needed a discreet friend to pick me up at the airport and drive me out to Echo Hill, the family ranch about an hour away. Then I could use my mother's old talking car, Dusty, to go the forty miles west to Utopia.

The discreet friend was there, all right. He was wearing the same old python jacket he'd bought thirty years ago in Singapore, and a pair of dark, Jackie Onassis sunglasses even though the sun was almost setting over the Texas hills. The discreet friend was named Dylan Ferrero. I'd met him in the peace corps in Borneo and he'd been the road manager some years later for my band, the Texas Jewboys. Dylan had a reliable but sometimes rather unsettling habit of only speaking in rock 'n' roll lyrics from the sixties and, on rare occasions, early seventies. He currently was teaching fourth grade in nearby Comfort, Texas. How he communicated with his students, I did not know. Now he was smiling and holding out his hand.

" 'Pleased to meet you,' " he said. " 'Hope you guess my name.' "

We drove west into the sunset, down I-10, which several biblical generations later would've spit us out in El Paso if we hadn't turned off after an hour at the first Kerrville exit. If you miss the first Kerrville exit you can always take the second Kerrville exit. There are only two exits to Kerrville off I-10 so you can't go very far wrong in the Hill Country unless you miss them both. Then you could wind up trying to bum a camel from the three wise men. If they were really that wise, of course, they probably wouldn't've missed the second exit.

" 'Little Deuce Coupe,' " said Dylan, who was inordinately proud of his vehicle. " 'You don't know what I got.' "

"I don't *care* what you got," I said. "I'm just glad you picked my ass up. I didn't know for sure I was coming until yesterday and I needed somebody I could really count on."

" 'Here is your throat back,' " said Dylan. " 'Thanks for the loan.' "

Though I loved him like a brother, I never had completely understood Dylan. I didn't even completely understand what the hell I was doing in Texas. So I just sort of set my ears back, puffed on a cigar, let Dylan and the road and the Texas night be my expert panel of shrinks and told them all that was on my troubled mind.

"I've been drowning in some deep waters in New York," I said. "I've been desperately but futilely attempting to find a missing autistic child who only says the word 'shnay.' "

" 'Shnay Mister Tambourine,' " said Dylan, oblivious to my torment, " 'sing a song for me.' "

"—so I was getting precisely nowhere and just banging my head against the wall and I decided rather sperm of the moment to come down here and see if I'd have better luck trying to locate a kidnapped cat. His name is Lucky. He's a three-legged cat that I found—"

" '—Read the news today, oh boy—' "

"You mean it's in the fucking newspaper?"

Dylan nodded. Maybe he was watching carefully so as not to hit deer crossing the highway or maybe he was merely at a temporary loss for lyrics.

"Anyway, I'll stay at Echo Hill tonight then head over to the Rescue Ranch in the morning. I'll see what's going on with Lucky's abduction and I'll pick up Mr. Magoo while I'm there and bring him back with me to Echo Hill."

" 'Me and You and a Dog named Goo,' " said Dylan.

"I'll tell you, I don't like what I'm hearing from Cousin Nancy. She's always very emotional but she usually has really good instincts. If she thinks some kind of foul play is going on in Utopia she's probably right. I just hope I have more success finding the cat than I've had finding the kid."

Dylan stared straight into the night, not taking his eyes off the winding road. When he spoke it was in normal conversational tones, but I recognized the lyrics as belonging to an old Bob Dylan song. Neither Dylan was all that far off base.

" 'Something is happening and you don't know what it is,' " said Dylan Clitorious Ferrero. " 'Do you, Mr. Jones?' "

"I sure as hell don't," I said, as Dylan drove us across the little causeway over Big Foot Wallace Creek and onto the main flat of the ranch. "All I know is that the missing little autistic kid is named Dylan."

Dylan parked the car beside the long white fence that seemed to go on forever in the moonlight. First he turned off the ignition.

Then he shook his head somewhat incredulously and shook a fag from his pack of Marlboro cigarettes, which he often referred to as "cowboy killers." Then he lit the cigarette and carefully recited the following words:

" 'Dylan, Dylan, Bo-Bylan, Banana Fana Fo-Fylan, Me Mi Mo Mylan, Dylan.' "

FOURTEEN

Long before David Crosby got everybody's liver, Crosby, Stills, Nash & Young sang that song about two cats in the yard or one cat on the roof and I can never remember which because I was busy at the time with Danny Hutton of Three Dog Night getting so high we needed a hook and ladder truck to scratch our asses. Echo Hill was my family's ranch, a camp for boys and girls in the summertime but only occupied by deer, jackrabbits, and twenty-five lonely horses who wandered around in the winter, waiting for the picnic suppers where the kids routinely fed them hamburgers and hot dogs and whatever else happened to be on the menu. The house where I lived when I was at the ranch was called the Lodge. It was over a hundred years old and was inhabited by the following sentient entities: two cats, Dr. Skat and Lady Argyle; one pet armadillo, Dilly, who usually but not always commandeered the backyard area; various species of field mice, spiders, and insects (even the cockroaches were friendlier in Texas); and my answering machine, which I checked like a hamster on cocaine.

After Dylan's car had circled the parking ring and headed back up the road to Kerrville, I stood for a moment alone in the little green valley in the moonlight. Alone with just the gentle hills surrounding me. Alone with the deer and the jackrabbits frolicking on the flat. Alone with the beautiful, blameless, cookie-cutter stars that you never saw in the city. Alone with the whippoor-wills, the bob whites, the owls, the fox, the coons, the possum, and several of Dilly's wilder cousins who would never think of coming in close proximity with those loud, giant, frightening, dangerous creatures known as men. There was a comforting peace and quiet in the little valley under the Texas stars and it seemed to tell me that I wasn't alone at all. I was, in fact, in some of the best company that I'd ever been with in my life.

It was not cold by New York standards. There was a great deal more space between manmade dwellings, between oneself and others, between people and the sky. Surely the whole world was a rescue ranch, I thought. Everyone was busy trying to save something. Some people saved money. Some spent their time attempting to save other people's souls. A few endeavored to save the lives of other creatures on the planet. A few even tried to save the planet. But the inexorable truth was that nothing could ever be truly saved. Like love, it could only be given.

There were large quantities of dried cat vomit on the living room floor of the lodge. Dried cat turds, too. As a detective, these somewhat unpleasant detriti more than anything else served as clues to inform me that Dr. Skat and Lady Argyle were obviously alive and well—quite alive and well from the look of things—and that Nelda, the woman from Medina who usually cleaned the lodge, had been following other pursuits of late, tending her goats or possibly resuming her long dormant career as an artist. Nelda was not without talent, and some of her earlier work currently hung on the walls of the lodge. Like everything else, of course, they were covered with cobwebs. Maybe she'd been preoccupied with moving into her postimpressionist period.

I set my suitcase down, turned on a few lights, and went immediately into the rather personal and laborious process of a man calling his two cats. Fortunately, there was no one around to hear except some of the night birds and a few of the more curious crepuscular creatures lingering around the Lodge. Whatever they might've thought, they kept it to themselves. Lady Argyle and Dr. Skat also did not respond. This always sent a shiver of concern through my being. I only had three cats in all the world. One was safely in the hands of a lesbian in New York. The other two were wandering around five hundred acres of Texas Hill Country at midnight and were not responding to my calls. This must be what it was like, I figured, when your children grew up and left home. I didn't have any children that I was aware of, thank Christ. It was traumatic enough having two cats who were not responding to therapy. Then, of course, there was another cat named Lucky. And where Lucky was in all this living hell of God and man's creation was anybody's guess.

I made some coffee, unpacked a little, then took a hot cup of Kona out under the stars and called Skat and Lady a few more times. There are those who will tell you that calling cats is a waste of time. They say that cats never come when they're called; they just show up whenever they feel like it whether you're calling them or you're fucking somebody or you've just dropped dead. It's all the same to the cat, they say. But, in all fairness to the cat, it must be vouchsafed that these three unnatural acts all do appear to look and sound a lot alike to the neutral observer.

By dawn's surly light, it may happily be reported, I was sound asleep with Lady sleeping on top of my head and Dr. Skat sleeping on top of my scrotum. They were creatures of narrow habit, and had, for example, Dr. Skat been sleeping on top of my head and Lady been sleeping on top of my scrotum, I would've known instinctively that something was seriously wrong. As it happened, something *was* seriously wrong, but it did not concern Dr. Skat or Lady Argyle. I did not learn the precise nature of the menace until late the next morning when I woke up in a moderate fog, made a fresh pot of coffee, took a cup and wandered into the Indian Ghost Room, and saw the red light on my answering machine blinking at me like a Gila monster with a facial tic.

FIFTEEN

There were two messages on the answering machine. The first was from Cousin Nancy who sounded like she was ready to commit suicide by standing on a chair and sticking her head through the blades of a slow-moving ceiling fan. The second message was from Rambam. He sounded like he was ready to shit standing. As all hell sometimes does, it had apparently broken loose in Utopia, Texas, and New York City simultaneously. Why all hell had chosen those two particular loci, I did not know. All I knew was that to answer these frenzied, frenetic messages on such a cool, crisp, clear, calm country morning amounted to a sin against God's creation. I took a few sips of hot coffee, looked out the window at the green, glowing hills, and realized that all of us were sinners. Some of us, I figured, just enjoyed it more than others. So I decided to deal with Nancy's neuroses first, then wrestle with Rambam's wrath if I survived the former call.

"Rescue Ranch," Nancy's recorded message screamed into my left earlobe. "We can't come to the phone right now. We're outside with the dogs."

I shouted the words "Cousin Nancy!" about forty-seven times at the top of my lungs and eventually Nancy, sounding somewhat winded, ran up the stairs of her double-wide trailer and picked up the phone. By that time, of course, I probably sounded somewhat winded myself.

"Cousin Nancy!" I said for the forty-eighth time.

"Oh, God, Kinky! I'm so glad it's you. Are you back at Echo Hill?"

"You don't hear any sirens in the background, do you? I'm either back at the ranch or I died and went to heaven, and if it turns out to be the latter I want to ask God whether or not it's really true that Marilyn Monroe dyed her pubic hair."

"While you're there you might ask Him to help us out over here. The devil's been workin' overtime in Utopia. How soon can you get over here?"

"I can meet you and Tony for lunch at the Lost Maples Cafe," I said. "We can be having a big hairy chicken fried snake by half past Gary Cooper time. How's that sound?"

"I hope it's not too late," said Nancy.

She sounded particularly shaky to me and I pushed her a little about the precise nature of the devil's recent activities in Utopia. She was extremely reticent, however, to reveal any details over the phone. She mentioned something about her phone being tapped and the neighbors having police scanners or some kind of other more sophisticated listening devices. I'd seen some of Nancy's neighbors briefly and they did not appear to be hi-tech spies. What I'd witnessed could be more accurately summed up as a *Deliverance* moment. Maybe all the pressure and harassment had finally pushed Nancy out where the buses don't run.

Three cups of coffee and two cigars later, as I was leaving the lodge for the Rescue Ranch, I noticed that Lady and Dr. Skat, possibly having observed the absence of my head and scrotum from the bed, now were curled up together sound asleep on the pillow. I thought fondly and fleetingly again of my cat, Cuddles, safe in

New York with Winnie Katz. She was my eldest. My firstborn. The silent, sensitive shadow of my conscience. But where was Lucky now? Where was Dylan Weinberg? Where were all the other disappeared ones who'd gone missing at the careless hands of fear or fascism or fate never again to return to that perfect pillow that was home?

SIXTEEN

From Echo Hill to Utopia is a hell of a drive for a 1983 Chrysler LeBaron wood-paneled convertible who's been sitting silently under the overhang of the Nature Shack all winter. It was the first time Dusty'd been out on the highway in quite a while and the steep grades and mountain passes from Medina to Vanderpool proved a worrisome challenge to her. The other minor problem was that all of her insurance and registration stickers were hopelessly out of date. Her license plate read 1-2-3-HOW! which was the way the kids at camp expressed their enthusiasm and appreciation for virtually anything, an extremely ubiquitous occurrence during the summer. The license plates had expired in 1985. That was also the year my mother had expired. Resultantly, it was the year I realized I'd never again be a completely happy camper. The good news was that traffic was usually very light on the road to Utopia and there wasn't much chance of your straining your pooper trying to give birth to a Texas state trooper.

As Dusty struggled up the steep slopes, so I struggled with the twin threads that had so recently become entangled with the fabric of my existence. As far as events at the Rescue Ranch were concerned, it was obvious that some of the "neighbors" had

indulged themselves in something of a campaign of petty harassment. They did not, according to Nancy and Tony, want to be living next door to seventy-six dogs. They would, apparently, have
rather been living next door to seventy-six trombones. Perhaps
understandably, they did not appreciate or support the work of
the Rescue Ranch, and their small-town gossip, innuendo, and
harassment had put Cousin Nancy in a high state of paranoia,
which was not a very difficult thing to do under normal circumstances. She was already quite paranoid from listening to Art
Bell's radio show all the time.

    Though it was probably cold as hell in New York, it was nice
enough here in the Texas Hill Country to put the top down on
Dusty. The mild, sunny weather and the majestic sweep of
breathtaking scenery could easily lull you into the narrow, misguided notion that all was well with the world. Many people felt
that way, no doubt, and many people were wrong. Many people
were always wrong. It went deeper than climate, geography, or
mortal circumstances. People just appeared to be born wrong.
That's why they kidnapped three-legged cats and little autistic
kids.

    Dusty had steamed and struggled and strived and finally
climbed the final peak on the way to Vanderpool, and now she
was gliding comfortably downhill toward the road to Utopia. I
put my mind into another gear as well and reflected briefly upon
the message I'd recently received from Rambam in New York. It
had not been as angry and as full of reprimand as I'd expected. If
anything, maybe he sounded a little disappointed. But compen-
sating for that was a tone that I'd heard before when Rambam
was seriously strapping on his lobster bib and getting into the
meat of a tough case. As I was driving to Utopia, he was already
interrogating Julia Weinberg at a dim sum meeting in Chinatown. He said he believed there was a peculiar dynamic between

the parents, Julia, and little Dylan Weinberg. He said he felt that Julia, either consciously or unconsciously, held the key to the kid's disappearance. How he knew this he didn't say.

It was a little after Gary Cooper time when Dusty and I hooked a left onto the Utopia road. It was a winding, rural road and the only eyes that watched us drive past belonged to goats and cows and horses. Their gaze was peaceful, nonthreatening, minding their own business. These local inhabitants were a welcome change after living in New York for so many months with two-legged animals.

We motored stately into Utopia, which was still a real town in Texas. The yuppies and developers and world-weary movie stars hadn't quite discovered it yet. It still looked like an outtake from *The Last Picture Show.* Paint was peeling off facades. Rust wasn't sleeping either. But dogs, horses, and even a few friendly people could be seen sleepwalking along the little town's colorful, not to say quaint, main street. The Lost Maples Cafe was in downtown Utopia on the left, and I parked Dusty somewhere in the middle of a gaudy necklace of pickup trucks.

Inside, the demographics were good; I was one of the youngest people in the place. Many of the patrons used canes and walkers to get around and wore old overalls and faded, weather-beaten farm caps. There wasn't a yuppie, a developer, or a movie star in sight. I was as close to an outsider as they were going to get, and even at that, most of the customers barely looked up from their chicken fried steaks and six-inch-tall meringue pies. I found Nancy and Tony already ensconced in a secure, secluded booth in the back of the place.

Nancy was wearing overalls and drinking a Mr. Pibb. Tony was sipping an ice tea and wearing a Willie Nelson "Born for Trouble" tank top. They seemed relieved that I had finally arrived in Utopia, but both of their demeanors also seemed strained and nervous. I sat down across from them at the table. After the salutations were exchanged and the food ordering process had been completed, I tried to get down to business.

"Suppose we take it from the top," I said. "Who do you think might've kidnapped Lucky?"

"Shhhhh!" said Nancy. Tony said nothing but he glanced around the room warily, like a character in *Day of the Jackal*.

"I mean we've got to start somewhere," I said. "Hell, it's already been in the papers."

"We're surrounded by enemies," said Nancy, in a whisper I could barely hear.

"You're serious?"

"They're all around us."

"In this room?"

Tony laughed. "No," he said. "She means our neighbors at the Rescue Ranch."

"Then why are we whispering?"

"It's a very small town," said Nancy in hushed tones. "Some of the parties involved could be right here in this restaurant."

"The people who took Lucky?"

"Shhhhhhh!" said Nancy.

SEVENTEEN

It's about a mile and a half from Utopia to the Rescue Ranch, and all of the way I worried about Cousin Nancy's sanity. Was it possible that a few crank calls and threatening signs and letters coupled with the abduction of Lucky the cat had made her a prime candidate for the Bandera Home for the Bewildered? Was the Lost Maples Cafe a nest of spies? Would anyone who called themselves a neighbor trespass on someone else's property to kidnap a beloved three-legged pet? Anything was possible, of course, but the patrons of the Lost Maples Cafe all seemed too geriatric for such nefarious adventures. Most of them were too busy adjusting their hearing aids and polishing their aluminum Jerry Jeff walkers and talking about the weather and dreaming their daydreams to ever consider embarking upon a nighttime mission, evil or otherwise. But according to Cousin Nancy, somebody had taken Lucky and now it fell to me, the big private investigator from New York, to find out who that somebody was.

Dusty and I followed Nancy and Tony down a gravel road and soon the Rescue Ranch came into sight. From the road you could see a nice-sized lake and beyond that the trailer where Nancy and Tony lived with ten dogs and, formerly, one cat. Off to the side of the trailer were large, airy, attractively fenced runs for the current occupancy of seventy-six dogs. At the moment, the whole place seemed quiet and peaceful. Tony got out to unlock and open the gate.

"Was that gate locked the night Lucky disappeared?" I shouted from Dusty.

"No," said Tony. "We never thought anybody would actually sneak onto the place, go into a trailer filled with dogs, and take a cat. It just doesn't make sense. Anyway, the trailer was locked but we found one of the windows open. Now, of course, we lock everything."

This was a long speech for Tony and I didn't want to ruin it by mentioning the old adage of locking the barn door after the cow, or in this case, the cat, had gotten out. I just followed them up to the trailer, parked Dusty, fired up a fresh cigar, and got out to meet some of my old four-legged friends.

The first one to hit me right in the scrotum at a hundred miles an hour was, as I expected, Mr. Magoo. Magoo divided his time between Echo Hill, when I was in residence there, and the Rescue Ranch. Living inside the trailer with Nancy and Tony, he had not become the goodwill ambassador to the outside dogs that I'd hoped he'd be. In fact, the outside dogs resented Magoo and the other inside dogs, and he was definitely persona non grata inside the dog runs. These fences were identified with colorfully painted signs that read: KINKY'S VIL-LAGE IRREGULARS, JOHN MCCALL'S WALL, WILLIE, LAURA (BUSH), DWIGHT (YOAKAM), ANN (RICHARDS), LAMAR (CONGRESSMAN LAMAR SMITH), LONE STAR BEER GARDEN, and various others who'd helped out the ranch from time to time. Magoo spent a good deal of his time standing outside these fences growling and snarling at the dogs inside who growled and snarled back at him. A goodwill ambassador, he was not. This was somewhat of a disappointment to me, like a father who'd hoped his son would become a famous military general and the boy decides to be a famous fashion designer. But what is life if not a series of small disappointments from which we rebound, pick ourselves up, dust ourselves off, and prepare to dream again.

"Magoo!" I shouted.

Magoo kept snarling in a most vicious manner at a large dog behind the fence. The dog's name, interestingly enough, was Cat, and it looked like a large hyena and it definitely could've eaten Magoo for brunch. Cat was a sweetheart, though. He was at the Rescue Ranch because his previous owners, total assholes, as far as I was concerned, had surrendered him to the pound for eating a social security check.

"Magoo!" I shouted.

Magoo, having already hit me in the scrotum and greeted me profusely, continued standing by the fence, snarling at Cat, who, for his part, seemed fully ready to tear Magoo's heart out. It wasn't a particularly pretty thing to watch. Fortunately, I didn't have to watch it long. Magoo suddenly ran across the yard, jumped into Dusty, and sat there waiting for my departure, which, unbeknownst to him, was going to be a while.

Nancy was in the trailer getting some things ready to show me, and Tony was making the rounds giving the dogs an afternoon snack. I followed him and got to greet some old friends and meet some new ones. Curly was doing much better. He was a black chow that could hardly bark because some fucking dog-catcher strangled him with a wire when he picked him up. Curly was just now able to wear a collar again and he seemed very proud of it. I saw some of the magnificent seven, the crazy and deaf Dalmatian named Helen; Fly; Roscoe, who was Robert Earl Keen's mother's dog and who came to us after she was bugled to Jesus; and the feral dogs from San Antonio with white-blue eyes that bore into your soul. The only human being in the world they trusted was Tony.

Once again I thought how much the place resembled a happy orphanage. These were strays, abused animals, dogs with backgrounds no one knew, yet they were happy, even joyous, to be at

Utopia with Tony and Cousin Nancy. You really couldn't blame them. They had all the love in the world.

By the time Tony and I went into the trailer, Magoo was still sitting in Dusty, and Nancy had arranged what she called "the evidence" all across the counter in the kitchen. There were two or three cardboard signs and a few threatening letters and notes. It didn't add up to much, but I wanted to hear what she had to say, so I grabbed a cup of coffee and sat down on the couch with four dogs under a picture of Roy Rogers, one of Cousin Nancy's heroes.

"These are all anonymous," said Nancy, "but we know who wrote 'em."

"And who would that be?"

"Our neighbors," said Nancy. "All the cardboard signs— there's three of them—were found on the gate, and they were all written in these block capital letters by Regina Wiggins who lives across the road. We even have a witness who saw Regina Wiggins putting one of them up. Her name is Josephine and she lives down the road."

"But Josephine is over eighty years old," said Tony, "and she can't see very well."

"But she swims a mile a day in the river," said Nancy, "and she's sharp as a tack."

"Who swims a mile in the river? Josephine or Regina?"

"Josephine swims a mile every day," said Nancy. "Regina's too busy putting signs on our gate. She also makes these horrible art pieces out of deer antlers and roadkill and tries to sell them at the local arts and crafts shows. She has a husband but no one ever sees him. They're retired taxidermists, I think. He's sick or something."

"These signs are sick," I said, getting up and studying Regina Wiggins's handiwork.

The first one read: YOU'RE OBVIOUSLY NOT CHRISTIANS OR YOU'D REALIZE DOGS ARE SIMPLY ANIMALS!

"Christianity raises its ugly head again," I said. "Give me a good old pagan any day."

The second sign read: WOULD YOU SHUT THOSE DOGS UP, PLEASE! THE NOISE IS UNBEARABLE! THINK OF YOUR NEIGHBORS!

"If Regina Wiggins had anything to do with taking Lucky, she's got bigger balls than Mr. Magoo."

"And we've got to get him fixed," said Nancy. This was a point of some contention, Magoo being the only unfixed animal on the ranch and me wanting to keep things that way.

"Give him a little more time," I said. "He's only four years old."

"He's already a deadbeat dad," said Nancy.

"Back to Regina," I said. "I think we can cross her off the list. She's way too open about this. She also seems educated. And I do admire her penmanship."

The third sign, also in neat capital letters, read: PLEASE MOVE AS FAR AWAY FROM HUMAN BEINGS AS POSSIBLE!

"I concur with her on that sentiment," I said. "Also we must give her an A for enthusiasm. She's very big on exclamation points. But I really think she's just a harmless crank. Let's not cross her off just yet—I just called her harmless. That's always a bad sign. Speaking of signs, what else have you got?"

Nancy walked to the counter and brought another note over to the coffee table, setting it beside the slumbering form of a large dog.

"Magoo usually sleeps on that coffee table," she said, "but he's still sitting in Dusty waiting for you."

"Well, he'll have to wait a little longer. This note—'You won't be so Lucky next time'—really interests me. For one thing, it wasn't done by Regina Wiggins. Not her style."

"It looks computer-generated," said Nancy. "Anybody with a computer could've written it."

I was about to agree with her when I felt the slight indentations on the back of the page. Clearly, it was not computer-generated. It was done the old-fashioned way. With a stencil. There weren't many people over seven years old who bought and used stencils these days. Probably only a few stationery stores sold them in the Hill Country. It might be worth looking into.

"I think I'll keep this note, if you don't mind. Now tell me more about the neighbors in the immediate vicinity whom you think could be implicated in this dastardly action."

"Well, there's Vernon Crabgrass and his wife, Uvula, who live right behind us. I think they're the ones who called the health department on us. Vernon owns a hardware store and Uvula hand wrestles a wild pig at the Annual Hogfest in Sabinal. Each year she wins and each year they give her a belt buckle. Vernon also calls himself a 'professional Christian hunting guide.' "

"They hunt Christians around here?" I asked.

"If they did," said Nancy, "they'd probably come home empty-handed."

"They say," said Tony, "that about six years ago some stray dogs wandered onto their place. That was four years before we got here, but I've heard the story from a number of reliable people. They shot the dogs and put all five of their heads up on their fenceposts by the road."

It was the middle of the afternoon, but I thought I felt a sudden chill moving through the trailer. All at once I had a strong urge to move as far away from human beings as possible.

"That's not nice," I said, unconsciously echoing the words Tony often used to reprimand occasional bad behavior amongst his flock.

"No it isn't," said Nancy, as she gently stroked Toto's head. Toto responded by growling at Yoda who'd gotten a bit too close.

"Toto!" said Nancy. Toto, without missing a beat, snarled again at Yoda, who totally ignored him.

"Moving right along," I said. "Are there any other good Christian neighbors who might have it in for the Rescue Ranch?"

"There's the Kilgores," said Nancy. "They're an old couple who live on the other side of us and they represent their manic-depressive son who's brokenhearted supposedly because he started a chinchilla farm on their land and he thinks the barking is discouraging the mating. But the Kilgores are pretty old. All they do is drive by in their old Buick every day at about two miles per hour, glaring at us from the road."

"Okay," I said. "Short of holding a seance, we're going to need more to connect the kidnapping of Lucky with the bad guys. We need more evidence, or witnesses—"

"Oh, didn't I tell you?" said Nancy. "There *are* witnesses! *Two* of them, in fact. While Tony was away at the vet, Wylie Skelton, in Leakey, my friend Cindy called and said she'd had car trouble and could I please drive over to her place, which is twenty miles away, and feed her two wolves."

If Tony was a man of few words, Nancy could really string them together like rosary beads. I didn't want to get in the way of her freight train of thought regarding the night Lucky had disappeared. I said nothing, relit my cigar, and she just kept rolling.

"It was just getting dark when Cindy called and I was smudging the trailer to ward off all the threats and bad vibes. An Indian friend once showed me how to mix the sage and the cedar and smudge a place and I put crystals in all the windows and mirrors outside the trailer to reflect the neighbors' bad thoughts right back at them."

"Good move."

"Anyway, the animals hate the smell and the smoke when I smudge the trailer so I opened the bathroom window for a while, then I closed it and locked the door as I left to feed the wolves at Cindy's. I said goodbye to everybody first and the last one I said goodbye to was Lucky. He was right there on the rocking chair when I left.

"It was a strange night and I kind of had a premonition that something bad was going to happen. Now I'd been out to Cindy's a bunch of times, and her two wolves are friendly and they know me, but on this night they both seemed to just go crazy when I arrived. They started howlin' and they just wouldn't stop."

"Was it a full moon?"

"That's another strange thing. It *wasn't* a full moon. It was really dark. So I fed the wolves and tried without success to settle them down a little, then I came back here and Tony was back but Lucky was gone."

"Was anybody else around that night?"

"Our friend Nancy Niland had come out from Austin and she came by and we all looked and looked for Lucky, but it was just so unlike him to run away, and then the next day we got the note. Do you really think you can find him?"

"Anything lost can be found. Anything found can be lost," I stated as I puffed pontifically on the cigar and pondered the situation. "You mentioned two witnesses?" I said at last.

"Yes! The first was Josephine—"

"Who can't see very well," interrupted Tony. "Especially at night."

"Well," said Nancy with some heat, "she saw good enough to spot a dark-colored van driven up to the front of the trailer and somebody comin' out carryin' something in what looked like a large burlap bag!"

"And she swims a mile a day in the river," said Tony.

"You don't believe her?" Nancy asked Tony.

"I believe she saw something," said Tony. "I don't know if she's sure exactly what it was."

"What about the second witness?" I asked, heading off the little tension convention.

"If y'all didn't like the first witness," said Nancy, "you're sure as hell not going to believe the second."

"Try me," I said. "Who's the second witness?"

"He's sittin' right out there in your car," she said.

EIGHTEEN

"I can't fucking believe it," laughed Rambam on the phone later that night. "Cousin Nancy says Mr. Magoo was a witness to the kidnapping of the cat? Let me speak to Magoo. I want to ask him a few questions."

"He can't come to the phone right now," I said. "He's busy licking his balls."

"He's a better man than I am. Jesus Christ! Does Cousin Nancy really believe this shit? She's gotta be cookin' on another planet."

"Well, she has been under a lot of pressure lately."

"*I've* been under a lot of pressure lately. But I haven't deposed the Taco Bell Chihuahua yet. Have you considered the possibility that Cousin Nancy might really be fucking nuts?"

"It has occurred to me," I said, thinking of the bad thought-reflecting mirrors on the outside of Nancy's trailer. "There are, however, certain rather compelling arguments that may indeed bolster her claim that Magoo might just make a viable witness."

"Not in Judge Judy's courtroom."

"Ah, but there is a higher law that is more righteous, true, and ethereal than any that could be contained within the courtrooms of men."

"Like I said, not in Judge Judy's courtroom—"

"Or women. Animals have been communicating with mankind for thousands and thousands of years. They've been trying to tell us things—"

"Like what? Take me out for a shit?"

"—and, sadly, and to our great eternal loss, most of us never listen and never hear what they're trying to tell us."

"You have about the weakest listening skills of anybody I've ever met."

"Ah, but listening to animals is very different from listening to some stultifyingly dull authority on some stultifyingly dull subject at some stultifyingly dull cocktail party—"

"Or stultifyingly dull phone call—"

"Anyway, when you listen to animals you have to listen with your heart. Cousin Nancy and Tony know how to do this. It's not something you can set out consciously to do. It's kind of like typing with your toes. And Nancy maintains that she's observed a major change in Magoo's behavior that began taking place the day after Lucky was kidnapped."

"He now pisses on your right leg instead of your left?"

"He now runs to the fence and barks furiously whenever a certain neighbor comes out in her yard. He never did that before."

"Who's the neighbor? Cruella DeVille?"

"No. It's a woman named Uvula Crabgrass and she hand wrestles a wild pig every year at the Annual Hogfest in Sabinal, Texas. She always wins and they always give her a belt buckle."

"You're making this up."

"I'm afraid not. And she'd be a good candidate for the catnapper. She's very vocal locally about her hatred of the Rescue Ranch. She sicced the health department on us. And there's an oddly recurring rumor about Uvula and her husband killing stray dogs some years ago and placing their severed heads on fence-posts along their property line."

"This is just too fucking crazy. I can't believe I'm even having this conversation with you. If this fucking woman hates dogs so much why did she kidnap a cat? Have you thought about that one, Inspector Maigret?"

"Maybe because cats don't bark. Maybe she'd read stories in the paper about Lucky being so important to the spirit of the Rescue Ranch. Maybe she thought it was easier to kidnap a cat and keep it against its will—"

"Oh, come on, Kinky. You don't really believe this fucking Uvula woman who lives on the neighboring ranch kidnapped a three-legged cat and is currently keeping it under lock and key in her dungeon and feeding it bread and water?"

"I didn't say I necessarily believed it. All I'm saying is that Magoo does."

It was now past Cinderella time in Texas. I was at my mother's old desk in the Indian Ghost Room of the Lodge. Magoo had finally stopped licking his balls and was now reclining comfortably directly behind me in his teenage bed, which also had once been my teenage bed. It had been passed on—and occasionally pissed on—in our family from father to dog for many generations.

"Okay, enough of this Texas bullshit," said Rambam. "Let's talk about something that's really important."

"Spit it."

"I think Julia Weinberg may be my future ex-wife."

This was potentially bad news and I should have seen it coming. Rambam was always a big hit with gentile Texas girls—in fact, with gentile girls everywhere. If they were good little Christian church workers, it was almost a guarantee that they'd soon be receiving Rambam's patented kosher meat injection. But what Rambam really wanted—what he desperately longed for—was a nice Jewish girl who fucked like a snake. Maybe because he wanted a Jewish girl so badly, it triggered some perversity in the Jewish girl's heart, if she had a heart. Anyway, he had all the Bubbettes he wanted but things never seemed to work out with that Jewish girl of his dreams. More important as far as I was concerned, if he hit it off with Julia Weinberg, who was attractive, intelligent, and Jewish, I could see him going totally off the rails in regards to the investigation. In other words, if he fell for Julia Weinberg, he might just decide to drag the case out just to keep her in his life. Rambam was a professional, but he was also human.

"Steve," I said, "don't let your feelings for this broad cloud your investigative instincts. We've got to find this black nanny Julia spoke about. We've—"

"I'm telling you as a friend," he said, "this girl might really be the one. She's gorgeous, she's funny, she's smart, and, last but not least, she's Jewish. Now all I have to find out is if she likes to be spanked. And the way things are going, I don't think that's going to take very long. I mean you heard it here first. I honestly can see her being the mother of my kids."

It was a strange and sudden role reversal. I'd been the one who had bugged out for Texas to look for the cat instead of the kid. Rambam had given me grief about it. My hope had been that in my absence Rambam would rise to the occasion. Apparently he had, but not in the manner I'd intended.

"Rambam, you're the one who said you thought Julia Weinberg, either consciously or unconsciously, held the key to the whole case. You've got to find that fucking key."

"I already have," said Rambam. "But it's not the key to the case. It's the key to my heart."

NINETEEN

It was a terrible turn of events. The last thing you wanted your private investigator in the field to do was become emotionally involved with a major player in the case. It could be argued, of course, that I was the one in the field. I was standing in one now, at three o'clock in the morning, throwing a yellow tennis ball to Mr. Magoo. There was nothing wrong with this really. Neither Magoo nor myself had to go to work in the morning or punch a clock or be anywhere at all for that matter except in this field.

I wasn't sure why the Rambam–Julia Weinberg thing was getting up my sleeve so badly. It could've been possibly in small part because of jealousy, I supposed. Julia was an attractive woman. I had been her hope and salvation briefly before I bolted for Texas. Now Rambam would be helping her through this traumatic period.

In a way it was like having your legs kicked out from under you. One minute you're free to float around the universe searching for missing three-legged cats because you think you've left a loyal, solid, professional, fox-hole friend in charge of things. The next minute the bastard falls in love and suddenly all bets are off and once again *you're* the one in charge of the sacred investigative quest.

"You'd think Rambam might be motivated to hurry up and find the kid," I said to Magoo, as I threw the tennis ball into the darkness for about the 119th time. "You'd think he'd want to impress the girl with his great missing persons' expertise. Find her little brother. Be her hero. But that's not the way he's playing it, believe me. He's playing it the same way you are. He wants to hold on to that golden tennis ball of young Jewish womanhood as long as possible before God or destiny or some bastard with a cigar throws it again."

For his part, Magoo had absolutely no interest in my metaphysical ramblings concerning Rambam and the Weinberg case. He chewed the ball ritually seventeen times and spit it out at my feet. Nothing mattered to him now but the golden tennis ball of God. If I'd dropped dead suddenly right here in the middle of the field in the middle of the night, Magoo'd probably be bouncing the fucking ball off of my head.

"You're a witness in a felony case," I said. "Surely, you of all people realize how important it is when you're in the middle of an investigation in the middle of the night in the middle of a field to remain objective about all parties in the case and to not become blinded by human emotions or turn into some kind of goddamn control freak."

Now, just as Magoo refused to release the ball until he was damn good and ready, my mind clutched the idea that I'd blurted out to Rambam hours earlier. Find the black nanny. I'd said it almost in the same instinctive fashion that Magoo employed to find a ball in the darkness. Why did the nanny seem suddenly important? Because we had close access to the parents and the older sister, and no one, cops included, had found or spoken to the person in the world closest to the world of the boy. Reading between the lines, I got the feeling that Hattie the nanny had been let go for the same reason that the health insurance hadn't been paid. Caring for this child had sucked the family dry, spiritually, emotionally, and clearly, financially, as well.

Maybe the nanny even had something to do with the kid's disappearance, I thought. Stranger things had happened. The kid going off with a stranger would even have been stranger. Kids almost never wander off or get abducted these days by total strangers. It's almost always somebody the kid knows and trusts. This kid hadn't known or trusted anybody in his short life except, of course, Hattie the nanny. Where was Hattie now? Maybe she was dead. Maybe I was dead and this was what Limbo was. Forever throwing a tennis ball into the dark and cold for a dog, for God, for country music, for Mom, for apple-fucking-pie, for freedom riders and taxi drivers and pen pals and popes and butterfly collectors and lighthouse keepers and little autistic children and three-legged cats wandering about lost and forsaken in this big crazy field where cactus grows out of eye sockets of dead Indians and the sky is paved with cowboy stars.

I willed Rambam to listen to his better angels and do what he did best, which was finding missing persons. Find the nanny and you'll find the boy, I found myself muttering under my breath. I'm the man who hates vacuum cleaners, but something keeps telling me this nanny is implicated. I prayed that Rambam would follow my urgings and not play this case out for the benefit of Julia. If that happened, before they found the kid they'd probably have a few little autistic children of their own.

As far as I was concerned, a woman's religion made absolutely no difference at all. Her ass was important, her legs, her brain, her heart, maybe a certain fetching crooked smile, maybe the way she waved goodbye. In fact, a girl I was going out with once asked Rambam if I was a practicing Jew. "If he is," Rambam had reportedly told the young girl, "he needs to practice a little bit more."

It was almost poignant when I thought about it. This big

macho Jewish guy like Rambam finding the perfect Jewish girl and falling in love. It was just too bad that it might come down to his finding love or his finding Dylan Weinberg.

The tennis ball was now laying on the ground in front of me, slick with dog saliva. Magoo was staring at it with a gaze and focus and intensity that was rarely to be observed in these parts. Very soon now I would be curled up with one cat on my head and one on my scrotum, and Magoo would be sound asleep on his teenage bed in the Indian Ghost Room. We both would very likely be dreaming of things that, no doubt, would be only dreams by morning.

TWENTY

"Pencils?" asked the old man behind the counter of the Old-Timer General Store in Medina.

"*Stencils,*" I said again a little bit louder. "Do you sell *stencils?*"

It was a bright, auspicious morning, but the campaign was not off to a flying start. On the other hand, I couldn't very well go into Uvula Crabgrass's house armed with a search warrant based upon the eyewitness testimony of a four-legged friend who was currently sitting out there in Dusty with a tennis ball in his mouth.

"You know," I said. "To make *letters.*"

"It *is* nice weather," he said.

"Forget it," I said. "Do you happen to have any of those Willie Nelson dimestore reading glasses?"

"Eating glasses?"

"That's okay," I said, starting to leave.

"You want to *pay?*" he said. "For *eating* glasses?"

"No, thanks."

"Sure we can fill up the *tank.*"

It was almost like talking to my friend Don Imus. As I walked

out the door, the man looked at me as if he'd awakened from a
deep reverie.

"You still want them pencils?" he asked.

It seemed that nobody sold stencils in the little stores in the
little towns around Utopia, Texas. So I drove on out to Utopia
itself, which I figured would take about two minutes to canvass
for stencils. By now the whole idea was beginning to sound
rather silly to me. There were other things I could've been doing
that would give me more bang for my buck, like checking the
bathroom window of Cousin Nancy's trailer, interviewing
Josephine, the dim-sighted, eighty-year-old witness who swam a
mile every day in the river, and speaking to the mysterious Nancy
Niland who just seemed to appear on the very evening that Lucky
had disappeared. The other possibility was to go back home and
masturbate like a monkey, which, from the general look of things,
would probably be just about as worthwhile an expenditure of
time as anything else I was doing.

It didn't take long to establish that the grocery store and con-
venience store did not sell stencils, and that Magoo was going to
be a major pain in the ass on this trip. He'd gotten it into his
head, quite naturally, I suppose, that I was taking him back to the
Rescue Ranch, to which he was not as yet prepared to reestablish
residency. This put Magoo in a high state of agitation, jumping
back and forth between the front and back seats of Dusty and fre-
quently draping himself across myself and the steering wheel,
which gave the humorous impression to anyone watching that he
was driving, but could also be quite dangerous. I didn't want to
be like the guy and the dog who hit Stephen King and almost put
him out of his misery. Like all authors, however, to paraphrase
Flaubert, Stephen King lived to dump a few more buckets of shit
upon mankind.

As a last ditch effort, I pulled up in front of Vernon Crabgrass's hardware store with the idea of maybe talking to the man. He wasn't there but the stencils were. If God had wanted man to sell stencils in hardware stores He'd have to put them there, and maybe He had. I wasn't sure that it proved anything, but it was suggestive. I bought a set that later I could use to compare with the note. I walked out of the store just in time to see Mr. Magoo hop out of Dusty and take a large dump on the street. Fortunately, this wasn't New York and I didn't have to follow him around with a plastic glove and a cellophane bag. Dog turds, like just about everything else in Utopia, were considered biodegradable.

Half an hour later, at the Rescue Ranch, Magoo having leaped out of Dusty to bark furiously at the dogs behind the fences, then returned stolidly to his station in the car, Nancy, Tony, and I took a brief walking tour around the trailer. There were two doors and four windows, and I found as we walked around that they all closed or fastened securely. At last we all stood in the backyard, with Toto and six of his friends surrounding us, and stared up at the bathroom window.

"What happened to the screen on this window?" I asked.

"It got blown away when the tornado hit about six months ago," said Tony.

"We all almost got blown away," said Nancy.

"Was this the window you opened when you smudged the trailer that night?"

"Yes," said Nancy a bit defensively, "but I'm pretty sure I closed it before I left and Lucky was there inside at the door when I left and I said goodbye to him and locked the door behind me."

"And that house on the hillside there?"

"Vernon and Uvula Crabgrass," said Nancy. "That's where she stands out in the yard and glares down at us."

"And it wasn't a full moon that night?"

"No, I told you, it was dark," said Nancy, almost on the brink of tears. "If I'd left all the doors and windows open, Lucky still wouldn't have gone outside. This is his home. The only time he ever leaves here is when sometimes Tony or I take him to town in the truck. He likes to ride in the truck. Oh, God, I wonder where he is?"

"Classic locked-door mystery," I observed.

"Unless Uvula was watching when Nancy left," said Tony. "Then she could've just come down the hill, forced open one of the windows, and taken Lucky."

"Then who drove up in the dark-colored van and took away something in the large burlap bag?" I asked.

It was a fair question, but it only added to the mystery. Maybe, I thought, Josephine would be more forthcoming when I talked to her.

"It was hard to get the sheriff to take it seriously," said Nancy. "To them it was only a cat. I don't know if somebody forced the windows or somebody copied the key or jimmied the door. All I know is Lucky was here when I left, and by the time Tony got back from the vet, he was gone."

"Classic locked-door mystery," I said, starting to repeat myself. There really wasn't a hell of a lot to go on anyway. Not for the first time since I'd come to Texas on this trip did I feel rather much like I'd been pissing up a rope. Either Lucky'd be back, or else he wouldn't, or else he'd gone to the happy hunting ground, in which case if you were an Indian you'd be visiting him some day beside the campfire smoke of the milky way, or if you were a Buddhist you'd run into him just the same only a little further on along the parade route. If you were a Jew like me, you probably wouldn't be meeting anybody anywhere, so you might as well learn to live with it.

I left the Rescue Ranch in a mild state of confusion and ennui, which I attempted valiantly to conceal from Nancy and Tony, who still held out some shard of confidence in my abilities as a mender of destinies. Finding a missing cat in the state of Texas is an enterprise that would challenge the greatest crime-solving minds in the history of the world. I had not as yet even been able to establish whether or not, indeed, a crime had occurred. All I knew was that a cat was gone and it'd taken along with it most of my charm. I was in a fairly black mood as I drove up the road looking for the rustic home of the dim-sighted—and for all I knew, dim-witted—octogenarian named Josephine.

"Of course I remember that night," said Josephine, who didn't look bad for her age—or maybe I'd just been in Utopia too long. "That was the night somebody kidnapped Lucky the three-legged cat. I read about it in the newspaper later. I just didn't know what I was seeing when I saw it."

"Describe what you saw again, please."

"Which time?"

"How many times were there?"

"I saw the same vehicle, a dark-colored van, come into the place twice that night."

"Keep goin', Josephine. You're doin' fine."

"The first time it drove up slow. The lights at the Rescue Ranch were off except the porch light, and I didn't pay too much attention for a while. Then I looked up and saw the person coming down the front porch steps carrying a burlap bag that appeared to have something in it. Then they drove away faster than they came in."

"And the second time?"

"It was a few hours later. But it was the same dark-colored van. This time all the lights were on and Nancy and Tony were home. You're not from the Utopia Sheriff's Department, are you?"

"No, I'm not."

"Didn't think so. You seem too smart to be a deputy."

"I don't know. The way things're going, that could be my next gig. Did the dogs bark?"

"Which time?"

"The first time."

"Of course."

"And the second time?"

"Of course. I should've known you weren't with the sheriff. They wouldn't be interested enough to send somebody around about finding a kidnapped cat. Where'd you come from?"

"New York. The only place where people are smart enough to come down to Texas to find a cat. Now, I know it was dark, but you say this person came by twice that night. Can you describe the person?"

"I never said the person came by twice that night. I said the same dark-colored van came by twice."

"I'm a little confused, Josephine. Maybe I've been living in New York too long. You're saying the same van came by twice, but two different people were driving?"

"That's what I'm saying, honey. The first time it was a man. The second time it was a woman."

TWENTY-ONE

My father, known affectionately during the camp summer as Uncle Tom, had stored a large cardboard box full of two hundred yellow tennis balls by the front door of the Lodge. This was perhaps a misguided effort on his part to jump-start the tennis program, which hadn't flourished at Echo Hill in over forty years. Now, every time Magoo entered or exited the Lodge, which was approximately nine thousand times a day, he'd stick his head into the box and conveniently come up with a tennis ball. The result was that soon the area around the Lodge was mined with yellow tennis balls that shone in the moonlight like large secular Easter eggs. From Magoo's point of view, of course, the box had been expressly placed there for his use alone. I didn't feel it was my place to belabor this point with him, but if we stayed down here much longer it might prove a trifle unsettling when Tom discovered there were only two or three balls left in the big box. I didn't let it bother me, though. I'd always felt that any game requiring more than two balls probably wasn't worth playing.

So as the days stretched into a week, and a sense of vast futility began to pervade my consciousness, I started to gauge my progress on the case and measure my purpose upon the planet by the level of the tennis balls in the cardboard box. When it got precariously low, whether I'd located Lucky or not, it would be time to go back to New York. There was still work to do, of course, and in order to be even remotely successful in my endeavors, I was aware that I'd have to borrow some of the focus and intensity that Mr. Magoo instinctively brought to the casino of ball playing.

Was I totally wasting my time down here looking for a lost or stolen cat? Was there indeed a more worthwhile pursuit in which any man could become entangled? Was the increasingly nagging notion that Rambam was quite literally flirting away the Weinberg case justified? These questions cried out for answers, like Dr. Skat crying out in the middle of night like a large Negro pelican. The fact was that Rambam was in New York and I was in Texas, so it stood to reason that I should deal with the case at hand, wrap it up as quickly and effectively as possible, and then cut buns for New York.

I already had, believe it or not, two very different theories for what might've happened to Lucky the cat, both appearing to be borne out by the facts as I knew them. There were still a few loose ends that had to be tied up with Cousin Nancy. And, of course, I still had to question Nancy Niland, whose number in Austin Cousin Nancy had provided. The hostile neighbors surrounding the Rescue Ranch would have to be interrogated as well. This, however, I felt could probably be accomplished in the course of one tedious Texas afternoon.

Everything could be done, I figured, in the space of a few days, but a still, small voice inside me kept telling me to take my time. It kept telling me that Lucky was alive, though very possibly in great peril. Like all still, small voices, it failed to tell me how to go about finding him. But there are accepted ways of finding a missing cat. You call for him. You look for him. You stir up the bushes.

And finally, when nothing is accomplished, you wait for a ransom note, for somebody to tell you they found a dead cat, or if you're very lucky indeed, for him to find his way back home. At least I had a plan for handling this case, I thought. That was better than the course of action Rambam appeared to have embarked upon. The only bush he seemed to be interested in stirring up was, very regrettably, attached to Julia Weinberg.

TWENTY-TWO

The next day started off with a fever of activity. For one thing, Dr. Skat had vomited during the course of the night. He had not, as one might expect, vomited upon my scrotum. Instead, the receptacle of choice had been my left cowboy boot, which I had placed precariously close to the bed the night before. How a cat can determine that you are left-handed is a wonder of nature that might provide some engaging and provocative subject matter for some graduate pinhead to spend seven years writing his dissertation upon. In this case, I merely let Dr. Skat out the back door so he could breathe some fresh morning air and nibble at the salad bar.

The boot, however, was more problematic. Never attempt to remove cat vomit, or cat turds for that matter, from any object until the particular detritus in question has fully dried. This only makes sense, if you think about it. Trying to remove the substance while it's still wet and viscous is a common mistake a lot of people make, to their eternal regret. Just take the object, in this case the boot, out into the sunshine and let it dry naturally. Later, using an old prospector's chisel and John Henry's hammer, it's easy enough to remove the foreign debris. Of course, if you are unfortunate enough to find that the cat has vomited upon your scrotum, this methodology is not really practical, for a number of reasons.

It was eleven o'clock by the time I'd dealt with Dr. Skat and the boot, and ground some coffee beans sent to me by my friend Kije Hazelwood in Kona, Hawaii. With a steaming cup of black coffee and a fresh Montecristo #2 cigar to keep it company, I went to my cluttered desk in the Indian Ghost Room and punched out the number Cousin Nancy had given me for Nancy Niland in Austin. The number had been changed to an unlisted number. I called Cousin Nancy to see if she had the new number.

"Rescue Ranch," she sang in a happy, high-spirited voice. Maybe she was bipolar.

"Nancy Niland's telephone's been changed to an unlisted number," I said. "Do you have the new number?"

"No. I don't. She did tell me something that I'm not supposed to tell anybody, but I think I can tell you. They think she has cancer. Isn't it terrible? Someone who's given so much to the Rescue Ranch and then something like this happens to them."

"Makes you wonder."

"Exactly. Well, I guess she didn't want a lot of people callin' her at this time, and I can certainly understand that."

"I can, too, but I've got to call her anyway. She may have important information about Lucky's disappearance. Do you know if she's married or has a boyfriend?"

"I think she said she lives with a guy. That's right. She said she's got three dogs and two cats and they all sleep in bed with her and, I would assume, the guy. She said there were twenty-four pairs of feet in bed at night. You can do the math."

"Since we're talking about cats in bed, Dr. Skat vomited in my boot this morning—"

At this point Cousin Nancy began laughing uncontrollably. It was possible, I thought, that she *is* bipolar. When the rictus of laughter subsided, about nine minutes later, I was able to continue with my sentence.

"—and I know you've got that new cat food from Hill's Science Diet. Didn't they give you about a ton of the stuff for free?"

"I'll give you a couple cartons next time I see you. It's a good thing Dr. Skat's with someone like you. If he did that around Utopia, most of the people would've given *him* the boot."

"Fuck the people in Utopia. Dr. Skat's a twenty-two-year-old Negro from New York, unless I lost a few years from cocaine. He came down here to Texas about seventeen years ago and he really needs that new Hill's Health Diet."

"Science Diet. Hill's Science Diet. By the way, how do you plan to be calling Nancy Niland if her number's unlisted?"

"We private dicks have our methods."

"Kinky, seriously, do you think you're going to be able to find Lucky?"

This question was asked with the pathetic innocence of a child. I did not have the heart to tell Cousin Nancy the truth.

"Of course, I'll find Lucky," I said. "Why do you think they gave me the corner bunkhouse?"

No sooner had I hung up with Cousin Nancy than I was on the blower with a pharmacy in Nancy Niland's part of town. Along with the now-dysfunctional phone number, Cousin Nancy had provided me with Nancy Niland's address, which I assumed was still current. If she was recently diagnosed with cancer, they'd no doubt be shoving a lot of medicine and painkillers her way already. Unfortunately, the pharmacy had no record of a Nancy Niland. They also had no record of a Dr. Schwartz. I told them I was new to Austin having just arrived in town from the Proctology Research Center in Buttflaps, Montana. Then we both hung up and I called another pharmacy.

The officious bastard at the second pharmacy I called also had no record of Nancy Niland and he evidently thought I was a real pill. By pharmacy number three I was starting to dislike pharmacists and Nancy Niland intensely. There was no joy there either. Then I called pharmacy number four.

"This is Dr. Schwartz," I said. "I'm calling regarding Nancy Niland, a patient of mine. Do you have her in your records?"

"One moment, Dr. Schwartz," said a harried-sounding woman.

She put me on hold and I listened to a saccharine Muzak version of "Cripple Creek" by The Band. I doubted seriously if Rick Danko would've approved, but it passed the time.

"Yes, we have her record, Dr. Schwartz," said the woman when she came back on the line, "but her prescriptions were written by a Dr. Stephen Worchel."

"He's my colleague," I said smoothly. "I'm just checking to see that all the information is correct. I have her address as 1893 Mockingbird Trail?"

"Yes, Doctor. That's correct."

"And what phone number do you have?"

Without dropping a pill, she spit out the unlisted number. I jotted it down in my Big Chief tablet.

"Yeah," I said. "That's the one I have, too."

TWENTY-THREE

I called Nancy Niland's unpublished number, got an answering machine, and left a message. I was not insensitive to the fact that it was not the best of times for her, but it was also not the best of times for me. Try chiseling dried cat vomit out of your left boot sometime and then driving to the Village of the Damned to interview three people of the lowest cunning possible on the troubled face of the earth. Even before I talked to them, I felt it was unlikely that any of Cousin Nancy's contiguous neighbors had kidnapped Lucky. Regina Wiggins, the Vernon Crabgrasses, and the friendly Kilgore family, aside from looking like they came directly from Dogpatch, all were on record for being highly vocal opponents of the Rescue Ranch. They all had the motive, of course, and they all had the means. But they also had the bare modicum of brains to realize that suspicion would almost certainly fall heavily upon them if they'd perpetrated such a dastardly crime. Not that they privately wouldn't have liked to. But nobody wants to be known as a catnapper. It's un-American. It's un-Christian. It's just about as low as being a dogcatcher. And everybody hates dogcatchers. God hates dogcatchers. Jesus hates dogcatchers. Even lawyers hate dogcatchers. And catnappers.

The point being, as I might've expected, these Nazi bastards fell all over themselves convincing me that they were not bad people. I told them I understood and, of course, I did. Building your dream home next to a dog ranch might not really be best foot forward for a lot of people. The Wiggins woman appeared to be somewhat out of touch with the mothership. Vernon Crabgrass was very possibly not the brightest bulb on the chandelier. His wife, Uvula, the wild-hog-wrestling champion of Sabinal, Texas, said "sometimes a dog's barking can cut into your soul." I thought at the time that it was a strange remark, but later that afternoon, driving back over to Cousin Nancy's, I realized that she might have a point. There are many things that can cut into your soul, and one of them might be driving down a country road one day and seeing the severed heads of five dogs geometrically arrayed upon the fenceposts. If these animals had been strays, *their* souls had now found a home in heaven. It was the animals who had done this to them who had strayed from the family of man.

Vernon had denied the incident outright with a shrug and a good ol' boy smile that somehow never managed to arrive in his glazed-looking eyes. Uvula did not admit to, nor bother to deny, the act had ever taken place. All she would allow was the phrase, "People talk." This was also true, and talking to a number of them in the town I could find some who'd heard rumors of the incident, but no one who'd actually seen anything. In itself, if verified, the primitive action did not automatically implicate the Crabgrasses in the abduction of Lucky. It was just something from the fairly distant past that might look good on their resume if they ever wanted to run for dogcatcher. The question I wanted answered was what had they done lately?

After spending some time visiting Nancy and Tony and the outside dogs and the inside dogs and the two potbellied pigs,

Arnold and Alice, I said what might be my final goodbye on this trip to the Rescue Ranch. As I was getting ready to leave, Arnold's former owners showed up as they did every Friday. They brought Arnold a large plate of lasagna. "Arnold," said Nancy, "*loves* lasagna."

On the drive back to Echo Hill, where I'd purposefully left Magoo on this trip, I realized that Nancy and I had both forgotten the new cat food she'd promised to give me. She could bring it over when she picked up Magoo, I figured. It was better for Nancy to pick him up at Echo Hill than for me to leave him at the Rescue Ranch. This cut down on the separation anxiety for both of us. As long as Magoo had his luggage, which was a tennis ball, he was always happy to jump into the Rescue Ranch truck with Cousin Nancy. If ever I had to leave him myself at the Rescue Ranch, he would cry and whimper unmercifully as I left and, invariably, this behavior would, well, cut into my soul.

After a hard day of investigative foraging along the one street and many backroads of Utopia, it was comforting to return to the peace of Echo Hill where Magoo and Lady and Dr. Skat, along with the horses that wandered freely around the flat, all seemed happy to see me. I don't mean strictly in the Mae West sense that all of them were running around the ranch with erect penises. I'm merely making the observation that animals have deep and strong emotions, too, and they can often miss someone as much as Johnny Cash.

I'd pretty well decided that I'd be heading back to New York in the next few days. Nancy Niland had not returned my call, but I could gather this important piece of the Lucky puzzle from her in New York just as well as Texas. Quite frankly, she was my last real hope in wrapping the thing up fairly quickly.

In the evening I set about doing a few ranch chores, like taking the trash out to the South Flat with Mr. Magoo in the Gray

Ghost. I also fed the horses, which was usually done by Nelda at this time of the year and by the camp wranglers over the summer. The horses' summer diet was always heavily augmented by hot dogs and hamburgers, which they shared with the campers at picnic suppers. I also arranged for Nelda, to continue taking care of the cats when I left. Nelda's theory was that the cats liked it best when nobody but them occupied the Lodge. Dr. Skat's projectile vomiting into my boot might have lent some credence to her theory, but personally, I believe the cats enjoy having a little company from time to time. Cousin Nancy would drop by to check on the cats a few times a week as well. Hopefully, she'd remember to bring the new cat food when she came to pick up Magoo.

Very late that night Rambam called me on his shoe phone from somewhere on the streets of New York. His voice was imbued with an almost adolescent tone of enthusiasm. I hadn't heard him sound that way in years. In fact, I'd never heard Rambam sound that way. As a semiprofessional mender of destinies, it was a particularly annoying thing for me to hear.

"So guess who I took to the River Café tonight?" said Rambam exultantly.

"Hattie Mamajello?"

"Who's that?"

"That's Dylan Weinberg's nanny who you were supposed to be tracking down."

"Who's Dylan Weinberg? Just kidding. The nanny moved to North Carolina a few years back. I'm working on it. I'm also working on Julia. Took her to Marionetta's for lunch in Little Italy."

"That's the place where your friend Alphonso treats you like Frank Sinatra every time you come in? That must've impressed her."

"Not really. But she liked the River Café. I think she also likes the ol' Rambino."

"That's what you're calling your penis these days?"

"Please. This is serious. We're taking it slow. I think we're going to Asti's tomorrow night. I've also invited Julia to join me on an upcoming case I've got in Belize. There's a man who's supposed to be dead who seems to be running a scuba school down there."

"How romantic. Taking her with you on a fraudulent death claim investigation."

"Oh, I think the romance is going pretty well. I'm not worried about it."

"I'm not worried about it either. I'm just worried about you getting off your Italian-Jewish buttocks and finding this nanny who seems to be the only person nobody's talked to who really knew this kid. Any good FBI profiler will tell you there's a high likelihood of her being implicated in this case."

"I hope an FBI profiler doesn't tell me about the moment of sudden intimacy that occurred today in the backseat of my car on the Staten Island Ferry."

"No kidding. Were you alone?"

"No, I wasn't," laughed Rambam. "And if things work out with Julia, I hope I'll never be alone again."

It was worse than I'd thought. Much worse. When I cradled the blower I turned to look at Magoo on his teenage bed with his kingdom of bones and tennis balls arrayed all around him. I turned back and surveyed my own kingdom of cobwebs and cigar smoke and blue coffee. It was about a quarter past time to get back to New York.

PART THREE

NEW YORK

TWENTY-FOUR

It was late Sunday night when the hack from La Guardia spit me out onto a windy and rainy Vandam Street. The lights were still blazing on the fifth floor, so I rode the freight elevator up to four, dumped my busted valise in the loft, waved to the puppethead, and legged it up to Winnie's lair to pick up the cat. I listened at the door and heard soft music playing inside but no voices. I knocked on the door.

"Who's there?" came Winnie's voice.

"Alice B. Toklas," I said.

Winnie opened the door wearing a rather revealing blue kimono and holding the cat in her arms. She was a handsome woman and the cat was a good-looking cat. They looked comfortable together. Neither of them looked very pleased to see me.

"So you stopped searching for the missing boy and you went down to Texas to search for a missing three-legged cat?"

"That's privileged information. How'd you know about it?"

"It's in the papers. Everybody in town knows about it."

It was a hell of a welcome mat, I thought. The damage, fortunately, was only to my ego, since I'd been keeping in regular touch with the Weinbergs even in Texas. I hadn't, of course, mentioned that I'd gone down there searching for a three-legged cat.

That might not play too well with the distraught parents of a
missing child I'd been hired to find. The mystery was how the
papers got hold of the story in the first place.

"Did you find the three-legged cat?"

"Not yet."

"Have you given up on finding the boy?"

"Not yet."

"Just for the record," she said, as she handed me the cat,
"you'll notice that all four legs are intact."

I thanked Winnie for looking after the cat. She said, "Don't
mention it," and closed the door. Then a man holding a mildly
irritated cat walked down one flight of stairs in New York City.

The loft seemed colder and draftier and gloomier than usual,
so I fed the cat some Flaked Tuna with Egg Bits in Sauce and went
back out onto the street to scavenge a little wood for the fireplace, feeling much like a character out of a Victor Hugo novel. It
seemed a little sad to be doing this, but not as sad as buying a
boutique bundle of four pathetic, hygienic little logs from some
corner store for twenty-seven dollars. I found a piece of driftwood
that looked like it had floated up from the *Andrea Doria*, and
nearby there was a broken wooden high chair. The baby had
either grown up or fallen off and broken his neck. Whatever'd
happened to him, he didn't need his chair anymore and I did.

The wood was a little wet, but I got the fire going, and pretty
soon the wood was crackling and the espresso machine was burping
along toward glory, and I was sitting at the desk calling Mike McGovern. The cat was sitting on the desk, very rigid and upright and self-
righteous, her back to me, of course, and her face to the wall.

"Did you find the three-legged cat?" asked McGovern when I
got him on the blower.

"Not yet," I said. "How'd they get hold of the story? I thought
I slipped down there fairly discreetly."

"Not discreetly enough apparently. The *Post* got hold of it. The last thing we ran was the 'Have You Seen This Boy?' picture and accompanying story that I wrote. But you didn't come out too bad on this deal. What's wrong with searching for a three-legged cat?"

"There's nothing wrong with it, McGovern. There's nothing wrong with searching for a three-legged milking stool. It just makes me look like a fickle, fatuous, fucking idiot."

"I'm not so sure about the 'fucking' part. It was a light-hearted piece. No harm done."

"Yeah, but who leaked the story? It might have implications on the investigation itself."

"I've already checked into that. You know how these guys are with their sources. About all I could get out of Eddie Klein—that's the guy who wrote the piece—was that his information came from 'a source close to the family.' "

I thanked McGovern and fortified myself with an espresso and a fresh Monte #2 from right out of Sherlock's ceramic cranium. I lit a kitchen match on the leg of my jeans and set fire to the cigar. Then I set the wheels turning in my own cranium. There weren't that many players in this game. Winnie knew I was going to Texas, but didn't know about Lucky. Chinga knew about Lucky, but didn't know I was going to Texas. Until just about the last moment, even I didn't know I was going to Texas. The only living soul in New York who knew I was down in Texas looking for Lucky was Rambam. Obviously, Rambam hadn't leaked the story to the press, but he might've told somebody who leaked the story to the press, and I had a fairly good idea who that somebody might be. The discovery would have to be handled with great sensitivity, however.

"Why the hell did you tell Julia about the three-legged cat?" I demanded, once I got him on the shoe phone.

"I didn't know the information was classified," he said. In the background I could hear someone singing an aria and an undercurrent of people laughing and a champagne cork popping.

"You're at Asti's," I said.

"Very good, Miss Marple. Are you back in town?"

"Winnie told me there was a piece in the paper about my going to Texas to look for Lucky. McGovern checked it out and it came from a source close to the family."

"I'm pretty close to the family right now."

"That's what worries me. Don't say anything in front of her—"

"No problem. I'm on my way to the men's room to look at the pictures on the wall and take a leak."

"That's just it. I think she leaked the story to the press."

"Why in the hell would she do a thing like that?" shouted Rambam defensively.

"That's what I want to know."

Soon the sounds of Rambam urinating like a racehorse could be heard over the blower. Julia knew something or had some agenda of her own, I thought. There was no rational reason for her to attempt to discredit me. I decided, for the moment, to keep those thoughts to myself.

"I don't mean to interrupt your ablutions," I said, "but how's the search going for the nanny?"

"Good news," said Rambam, brightening. "She's back in New York as of today. Apparently, North Carolina had changed in the forty-five years she'd been away. Hattie didn't like it, so she came back. She's going to be staying with her older sister in Harlem. The sister's about ninety-six. I talked to her today. She says Hattie's been having some scary dreams about the boy."

"So in spite of your frenzied social calendar you've been able to get some work done. You've proved once and for all that you can walk and chew gum at the same time."

"I've also proved that I can take a whiz and talk on a shoe phone at the same time. When do you want to meet with Hattie?"

"What's wrong with first thing in the morning?"

"No can do. Dim sum with Julia."

"Okay. How about tomorrow afternoon?"

"Look. I promised her I'd take her to Coney Island tomorrow afternoon. She's lived in New York her whole life and she's never been to Coney Island."

"*I've* never been to Coney Island."

"You poor, culturally deprived Texan. I'll take you some other time. Let's interview Hattie tomorrow night. Going to Harlem at night is almost as good as Coney Island."

"So how *is* it going with you and Julia?"

"Speaking of which, I've got to get back to the table. But let me tell you something. If it were going any better, I'd think I was living in a fucking fairy tale."

After I hung up with Rambam, I stared for a while at the cat, who was now curled up under the heat lamp on the desk. I puffed on the cigar a bit and watched the lazy smoke drift off to dreamland.

"You are, brother," I said.

TWENTY-FIVE

The next morning I made three phone calls and I was through for the day. I made one to each Weinberg, excepting Julia, whom I knew was busy dancing the light fantastic with Rambam, and one to Nancy Niland. I told the Weinbergs that we'd located Hattie and were pursuing a new line of thinking concerning the investigation. They both responded in the manner of extras from the cast of *Coma*. Possibly they'd read the newspaper account of my hiatus to Texas to look for Lucky. For whatever the reason, their enthusiasm, confidence in my crime-solving abilities, and spirit in general seemed lower than two tandem whale turds left over from the Iconoclastic Age in the Iphigenian Sea.

Nancy Niland was on her way to the doctor's and didn't have a lot of time to chat. She said she was sorry she hadn't called me back. Things were crazy. I said I understood. I said I'd call her back. She asked if Lucky had turned up. I said not yet.

Nancy Niland had some explaining to do, but I didn't want to interrogate her until I could keep her in my sights for a few lucid moments. Right now I was operating on the very real possibility that she and her male friend had, for reasons still to be determined, taken Lucky. There could, I supposed, have been another explanation for the events seen by Josephine, but at the moment I tended to believe she was a very creditable witness. Not taking anything away from Mr. Magoo.

I called Cousin Nancy to compare notes one more time on Nancy Niland. What had been Nancy Niland's attitude toward Lucky, I wanted to know? Nancy said she loved Lucky. On one of her trips to the Rescue Ranch she'd even asked if she could have him. This was sounding better and better. But Nancy Niland wouldn't have taken Lucky. She loved Lucky but she loved the Rescue Ranch, too. She'd put in a well for the ranch. She'd donated money.

"And you saw her the night Lucky disappeared?" I asked.

"Yes," she said.

"And have you spoken to her since?"

"No, she'd gotten an unlisted number."

Like a dog with a tennis ball, I refused to let go.

"What did she seem like that night?"

"She was a very calming influence on us. She said she knew Lucky'd be all right and he'd come back."

"And she hasn't called you since to find out?"

"No," said Nancy, "but she's probably been going through hell with her illness. That's probably why she changed her number."

"Probably," I said.

Not only was Rambam at the mercy of his penis but, apparently, I was, too. I couldn't effectively move on the Hattie Mama-jello situation until he picked me up that night. I didn't even know how to get to Harlem and I wouldn't go up there at night anyway without the entire Polish Army.

So, in a moment of weakness, hunger, and possibly nostalgia, I called Ratso and enticed him to join me in Chinatown. It was fairly easy to entice Ratso to go to Chinatown. He loved the Kinkster. He loved Chinatown. And he loved not having to pick up the check. Unfortunately, Big Wong's was closed on Mondays. So we tried out the new place with the old waiters on the other side of Canal Street, Wing Wong's.

"Did you find the three-legged cat down in Texas?" was the first thing he asked me as we stared across two steaming bowls of *won ton mein* soup.

I sucked some noodles for a while, which is usually a good stalling tactic because the noodles in Chinatown are very long noodles. You can't eat little bites of a long noodle. You've got to suck up a large portion of it and there's going to be an accompanying sucking sound, which has nothing to do with either homosexuality or Ross Perot. That's just the way it's been done for centuries before autism was diagnosed, before there were Christians or Jews or Muslims or Rescue Ranches, back when all of Manhattan looked like Central Park without the roller bladers, back when doctors drove Buicks. I tried to explain this mandatory noodle-eating sucking sound once to the former Miss Texas, 1987, but she didn't want to hear it.

Ratso didn't particularly want to hear it, either, it seemed. He was waiting for an answer. I figured if I was going to discuss any work-related matters with him, it would be wiser to discuss the disappearance of the cat rather than the kid. It would be harder for Ratso to fuck things up in Texas. It'd be quite easy for him to fuck them up in New York. And yet, I had to admit, he did provide a few eccentric angles and a Dr. Watson-like, human sounding board to any investigation. He also, unfortunately, provided a great deal of tedium.

"So did you find the three-legged cat in Texas?" he persevered.

"Not yet," I said.

"Why not? You were down there a week."

"Because Texas is a very big state, Ratso. It's hard to find a little cat in a big state."

"If Alaska were divided in half, Texas would be the third-biggest state."

"Ah, but Watson, Lucky wasn't missing in Alaska. That would've made the case even harder, not to mention colder."

"So did you round up the usual suspects?"

"The usual suspects usually are a wash, Watson. I think they'll prove to be in this case, as well. There's a small group of local neighbors who wish the Rescue Ranch would go away, but somehow I don't see any of them breaking in and kidnapping a cat."

"Any eyewitnesses?"

"Two."

"Well, there's a start. Who are they?"

"One of them has four legs, chases tennis balls, and is widely regarded by me to be my best friend. Present company always excluded, of course."

"You're fuckin' kidding. Mr. Magoo? You took time off a major manhunt for a missing child to go to Texas and look for a cat, and the key witness is a dog?"

"That's about the size of it. There is another witness, however. A woman named Josephine who seems pretty sharp for her age."

"How old is she?"

"About a hundred and ninety-seven."

"Okay, so she's old. Kids on the street today think we're old. If she's old and sharp, she's probably a good witness. What'd she say she saw?"

"The night Lucky disappeared, she saw a dark-colored van come in the gate and pull up to Cousin Nancy's trailer—"

"That Cousin Nancy. She's the one you told me about before? Thinks UFOs or satanic cults may be involved?"

"I haven't ruled them out, either. Anything's possible in Texas.

Anyway, the van pulls up, a man gets out, and here Josephine is distracted for a brief time—"

"Maybe she went to take a Nixon."

"Very possibly, Watson. Your earthy humor is always appreciated as a leavening agent in any investigation. Anyway, when next she observes the situation, the man whom she saw getting out of the van is coming down the front steps of the trailer with a burlap bag in his hands. Then he drives away. Only the porch light was on, and Nancy and Tony, her husband, were gone when the intruder came."

"Did the dogs bark?"

"Ah, Watson, but of course. Then, a few hours later, once Nancy and Tony are back and discover Lucky's missing, the same dark-colored van comes back. This time it's driven by a woman. It's Nancy Niland, a benefactor of the Rescue Ranch from Austin, a professed great admirer of Lucky, and a woman who's recently been diagnosed with cancer who—"

"Aha!" Ratso ejaculated rather loudly. The patrons of the little restaurant gave him a brief, collective curious glance. "They've forgotten the ginger sauce again!"

Ratso remedied the situation with the waiter, paused until the appropriate sauce arrived, then gave me a gaze of great gravity.

"That's it, don't you see? It's Patsy Ramsey all over again!"

"I'm afraid I don't see, Watson. All I see is a large Jewish man eating a gross amount of Chinese food."

"When people are diagnosed with a life-threatening illness, they begin to get closely in touch, possibly for the first time, with their mortality. This, plus the drugs that're probably already being prescribed, often pushes even a well-balanced individual over the edge. That's what happened with Patsy Ramsey. She had ovarian cancer, took heavy dosages of painkillers and tranquilizers and antidepressants and who knows what else, and she just—"

"Started cookin' on another planet?"

"That's it, Sherlock. Look no further. The woman from Austin is the culprit, I'm certain. She had an accomplice, of course. Did you check to see if she has a husband or boyfriend or male companion of some sort?"

"Yes, I did, Watson, and yes, she does."

"Have you interviewed her?"

"Just contacted her for the first time this morning. She'd gotten an unlisted phone number. She hasn't even called Cousin Nancy to see if Lucky's been found."

"That's it!" shouted Ratso triumphantly. "Case closed!"

"For once, my dear Watson, I'm almost inclined to agree with you."

"Now, are you getting any closer to finding that lost kid?"

"Not yet," I said.

TWENTY-SIX

The rest of the afternoon was pretty much of a wasteland. I thought about tidying up the loft a bit, but it was a hopeless task and, like the tree that fell in the forest, I questioned the validity of cleaning the place if nobody was ever going to see it. Instead, I had a few hefty shots of Irish whiskey, relit a dead Cuban soldier, and sorted through a few letters, a few bills, and the occasional misguided wedding or bar mitzvah invitation. Then I went over to the living room and reclined on the davenport for sort of a pre-Harlem power nap. The cat wandered over, and, in an unusual display of affection, curled up beside me, placing her head on my shoulder. We stayed like that for a while, but I couldn't sleep. So I told her a story.

More people than you'd think tell stories to animals, and animals absorb more from the stories than most people think. They may not understand all the words, but they pick up the tone and the coloring and the flavor, and I believe they remember the story. Children, on the other hand, expect you to tell them stories, so they don't really listen with their hearts, which is just as well because those stories usually aren't that good anyway. And the kids often think the story's just for them, but it's not just for them. It's just a story.

"This is a story," I said, "from a book I once read by Elizabeth Coatsworth called *The Cat Who Went to Heaven*. It won the New-bery Medal in 1931, I believe. At least it won some fucking award either then or in 1939 when Hitler was on a roll and I wasn't even born yet. Winning the Newbery Medal in 1931 is not what it used to be. It's a little like being Miss Spiritual Tramp, 1948. Or Miss Texas, 1987. As time passes, people want to know what you have done lately and, of course, nobody's done shit lately. The men are too busy dreaming of the girl next door who always grows up to be a lesbian, and the women are all still waiting for their knight in shining armor who usually turns out to be an investment banker with a three-inch dick. Are you with me so far?"

The cat was clearly hooked. She lay still on the davenport, her eyes looking into mine. I continued the story.

"There was this very poor artist in Japan in the old days. Those're the same people who gave the world sushi and karaoke. Anyway, one day the town priests gave him a big commission to paint a large picture of the Buddha for the temple. He knew he had to do his best work, because if the priests liked it, it would keep him in octopus beaks for a long time, or whatever the hell those people ate.

"He decided to paint the Buddha with all the animals coming up to him in a line, from biggest to smallest, starting with the elephant. The artist found a story about how the spirit of the Buddha had once traveled in the elephant and these men were dying of starvation in the Ferlinghetti Desert and they stumbled upon the elephant and asked him if he knew of any food and the elephant said just go a mile over that way and you'll find a dead elephant at the bottom of a cliff. Then the elephant took another route, went on ahead of the starving men, and jumped over the cliff."

The cat was rather at a loss over this part of the story. She was certainly not a Buddhist. No self-respecting cat is a Buddhist. They are often Episcopalians or something equally pragmatic.

"So while he's painting this beautiful, compassionate elephant, a little stray white cat walks in and the starving artist doesn't have much sushi but he shares what he has with the cat and then they both sing a few karaoke numbers. The stray cat has found a home with the artist and the artist has found a worthy companion in the cat for the lonely job ahead. As the days pass, he paints more animals—a water buffalo, a horse, a donkey, a deer, a dog. Each animal is a masterpiece, and this is beginning to get up the cat's sleeve a bit. When the hell's he going to paint *me* in the picture, she wonders? If the truth were known, the cat was becoming somewhat jealous of all the other animals in the bar mitzvah reception line to greet the Buddha."

I could tell that the cat was starting to empathize with the little white cat in the story. Her eyes were blinking and her tail began swishing rather violently, sure signs of irritation. And I was just getting to the part that I knew she really wasn't going to like.

"It must've been really unpleasant for the little white cat to have to sit there watching this Japanese nerd painting virtually every occupant of Noah's Ark and leaving out the cat. But what the cat didn't know and the artist did was that the Buddhist religion discriminates against cats. They'll put dogs and rats and dung-beetles and even human children in pictures with the Buddha, but you'll never find a cat. This is because thousands of years ago, when the Buddha had a midlife crisis and was wandering around in the forest looking for his grandmother's house, all the animals came over to comfort him except the cat. The cat, according to legend, was too independent to come over to the Buddha. Maybe he was too busy. Maybe he was working on a few projects. Maybe he just didn't give a damn about visiting a fat guy with a ponytail sitting under a tree. But the Buddhists, who are supposed to be so kind and spiritual and understanding, never forgave the cat. For five thousand fucking years they never let the image of a cat be seen in a picture with the Buddha."

You don't often see a sad-looking cat but when you do, it can be truly heartbreaking. Just like no one's ever been able to train a wolf to sit, no one's ever seen a cat cry. But they do grieve. They silently weep. And just like the rest of us, they weep for themselves.

"The artist felt terrible for the cat. He'd taken her into his humble cottage, fed her, and in a certain, special way, the little white cat had become his confidante and his best friend in the world. He tried to tell her, but she didn't understand. The priests were very strict about this rule. That's why some call it dogma. If the artist were to put the cat into the line with the other animals, the priests would refuse to pay him and cast asparagus upon the painting. He'd never work in that town again. He'd no doubt starve to death. He just can't do it. He wants to live! He wants to paint!"

The cat, indeed, looked very sad. I wondered what perversity in the architecture of my being caused me to tell such a sad story to a cat. But it only got sadder.

"The little white cat sat next to the starving Japanese artist and watched him put the finishing touches on his masterpiece, and the little white cat was so terribly sad, not understanding how ignorant and vengeful and harmful even the most well-intentioned of religions can be, and the starving Japanese artist saw how very much she wanted to be in the picture and he shouted fuck the priests and he began painting a beautiful likeness of the little white cat in the space that was left at the end of the line of animals coming to greet the Buddha. When the work was completed, he knew he was finished in more ways than one.

When the cat saw herself in the completed painting, her little heart was so filled with joy that it could not contain itself and it burst and the little cat died."

Now the story was starting to make *me* sad. The cat, however, seemed to be handling things in a stoic manner. But her eyes did not look like Christian eyes anymore. They did not seem to really believe in the goodness of man. They looked strangely Jewish— like they didn't trust people anymore. Cats, of course, are like that.

"The starving Japanese artist, who by now weighed about seventeen pounds, buried the little cat in the garden and he built a little wind chime made of seashells for her. Afterward he covered the painting and had it delivered by special ox cart to the temple where it was mounted on the temple wall. When the priests unveiled it, they just about shit standing. They pointed to the little white cat at the very tail end of the long line of animals meeting the Buddha, and they shouted, 'This painting is horribly flawed! The artist must be punished for this sacrilege! Everybody knows there must never be a cat in a picture with the Buddha!' And they covered the painting up with a large black curtain and stormed out of the temple in a parochial snit."

I could see I was losing the cat. Her attention span had never really been her long suit, and the story had already gone on about four hours longer than I'd intended, but now, thank Christ, or bless the Buddha, it was almost over, and I felt compelled to finish it even if a nuclear bomb fell upon the city and turned our eyes to jelly and left two charred sets of skeletal remains on the davenport. I believe you should finish what you start in life as much as possible, not to mention that it's always good to read a story from a book that's older than you are.

"So the next day half the fucking town was gathered in the temple along with the priests and the artist to determine what should be done about this irreverent, flawed work and the man who created it. The heavy black curtain was taken down from the painting on the wall of the temple and the priests and the artist now stared at the painting in shock and wonder. High up on the temple wall, where no man could touch it, the painting had magically changed overnight. The little white cat had vanished from the end of the line of animals waiting to greet the Buddha. She had moved to a new position. She was now curled up comfortably, sleeping, directly under the hand of the Buddha."

As I finished the story, having practically moved myself to tears, I was aware that the cat appeared to be demonstrably disinterested. I suppose I had told the story in the first place in order to justify to myself the time I'd spent in Texas looking for a cat instead of a kid. The cat stretched and yawned and went over to the window to watch the darkness descend upon Vandam Street. I refused, however, to be judgmental about the cat. You never know what someone takes away from a story.

It was still a few hours until the time Rambam was picking me up to go interview Hattie Mamajello in Harlem, so I put on my hat and my coat and grabbed a fresh cigar out of Sherlock's head and headed for the door. I left the cat in charge.

The evening was getting quite chilly, but the wind and rain and clouds had cleared off and as you walked down the streets of the Village you could almost see the sky. It was better than walking in midtown. There, walking between the buildings often reminded me of Oscar Wilde's poem the *Ballad of Reading Gaol*, in which he describes "that little tent of blue we prisoners called the sky." Tonight it looked like they'd pretty well folded the tent.

I bought a newspaper, some cat food, and a cold hero sandwich and headed back to the loft to wait for Rambam.

I was sitting at my desk waiting for the espresso machine to finish the *1812* Overture, and puffing a cigar, when I opened the paper and saw the story on the bottom half of page one. At first, I thought I'd been drinking. Then I realized I *had* been drinking, but the story was still there.

So I called Rambam.

"It doesn't look like we're going to Harlem tonight," I said.

"Good," said Rambam. "I'll just stay here with Julia."

"Why don't you go out and buy yourself a newspaper."

"Because I can't go out in the street naked to buy a newspaper."

"Too bad. The story's on page one of tonight's edition of the *Daily News*."

"Hum a few bars."

"Okay. How's this? Hattie Mamajello was murdered this afternoon. Somebody pushed her off a subway platform."

TWENTY·SEVEN

In a little less than an hour, the cat and I observed a shiny new Lincoln Continental pull up beside a line-dance of garbage trucks on the street below. A familiar form stepped out of the Lincoln and walked over to an area of the sidewalk directly below our perch. The next thing we heard was a shout that carried on the night air like the cry of a large leather-winged bat.

"Throw down that fuckin' puppethead!" shouted the voice. The cat and I looked at each other.

I went over to the fireplace mantel and procured the puppethead and went back over and opened the window and threw it out into the blameless night. The parachute billowed brightly in the light from the street lamp. Rambam circled neatly, made a minor adjustment, and came up with a clean catch. Moments later, with a knock on the door, in came Rambam's big head and the puppet's small head, which he casually flipped to me like one of Magoo's tennis balls.

I took the little black head over to the mantel and placed it carefully back on its perch. "Another fine job, Yorick," I muttered as the puppethead graced the loft with its guileless, high-beam smile.

"That's just fuckin' great," said Rambam. "We've got a murder on our hands and the guy I'm working with is carrying on a
conversation with a little wooden puppethead."

"I wasn't conversing with the puppethead," I said. "I was
complimenting the puppethead. There *is* a difference."

"Nine out of ten doctors at Bellevue might disagree with you.
Where's the fucking newspaper?"

"On the desk," I said. "Under the cat."

He went over to the desk and unceremoniously shooed the cat
away and rapidly read the story of the lonesome death of Hattie
Mamajello. It wasn't all that lonesome, you might think, with
hundreds of people around. Yet everybody believes that death is
always lonesome. Let me know when you find out.

"Mother of God," said Rambam, "you never told me the crime
occurred at the Battery Park subway station."

"Why is this station different from all other stations?"

"Because it's in Lower Manhattan. It's right near Wall Street.
It's two blocks from the fucking stock exchange."

"So?"

"So don't you think that it's a little strange for a black nanny
from North Carolina, without any education and without any
current employment, to be hanging around in that district?"

"Well . . ."

"What do you think she was doing? Checking up on her
investments?"

"Whatever she was doing there, I'll tell you what it indicates.
It indicates to me that she was somehow involved in the disappearance of the boy. Maybe she knew too much or wasn't playing
along or was double-crossed by her coconspirators. I think we
need to go to the police."

"And I think we should go to Battery Park."

"But aren't we taking a risk not sharing this information with the cops in such a sensitive, high-profile case? Isn't it illegal or something to conceal Hattie's identity from them?"

"The only thing illegal is I double-parked the car. Let's go."

Rambam flipped the paper back onto the desk and headed for the door. I put on my hat and coat again and grabbed a few cigars for the road. For the second time that night, I left the cat in charge.

We hopped in the Lincoln and the vehicle took off like a sleek urban shark. Rambam drove fast as hell with a measured confident insanity like all good little New York motorists. Everybody was in a hurry to get somewhere and, of course, so were we.

"This is a nice car," I said. "Where'd you get it?"

"You know that scuba instructor in Belize who's supposed to be dead? He doesn't know it yet but he loaned it to me."

"That's very nice for a guy who doesn't even know he's not dead."

"There's a lot of guys like that," said Rambam, narrowly missing a wayward Indian cab driver. "I'm trying not to be one of them myself."

"Look," I said. "What're we going to do when we get to the Battery Park subway station? Recreate the accident or something?"

"That's not as stupid as it sounds. Going back to a scene of a crime or accident on a subway or a busy street corner the next day at the same time it occurred is a good way of digging up additional witnesses. We don't really have that luxury here. Whoever killed the nanny is on the move. And don't expect to see any crime scene tape or anything here. They probably closed it off for about an hour then packed it in because rush hour was coming. Nothing stops rush hour but the return of the messiah."

"How do we know that a black nanny from North Carolina wasn't the messiah?"

"Because Vegas has it six-to-five that she was the Antichrist."

Rambam performed an O.J. Simpson parking job about five feet from the curb near the entrance to the subway station. He took some kind of special parking permit out of the glove compartment and tossed it on the dashboard.

"This'll probably be a lot of hurry up and wait, you understand. Roughly two hundred thousand people go through this station every day—"

"With emphasis on the word 'roughly.' "

"—and the transit cops have probably already interviewed every witness they could find. If the subway gods are with us, they might even let us have a peek at the file on this one. Or they might try to refer us to Homicide South, which would just be a waste of everybody's time. There she is, by the way."

"There who is?"

"The lady whom millions of people who've lived here all their lives have never even bothered to see."

In the middle distance out in the harbor, framed against the sea and the sky, stood the Statue of Liberty.

"I wonder," said Rambam.

"You wonder what?"

"If she was looking down in the subway at two-forty-five this afternoon?"

TWENTY-EIGHT

Rambam was right about there no longer being any crime-scene tape in the subway. Rush hour had come and gone, but it still seemed as if 200,000 people were—in the words of Jimmie Rodgers, the Singin' Brakeman himself—"waitin' for a train." If we hadn't read about it in the paper, we never would've known that Hattie Mamajello's last moments of life had taken place here on this platform. A train was coming in now and I unconsciously found myself taking a few steps back from the edge of the platform and furtively looking around me. But whoever'd shoved Hattie to her terrible death was long gone, and so, very likely, was everybody else who'd been on the platform at the time.

In the transit precinct office, sitting behind a small desk cluttered with paper, was a transit cop. The plaque on his desk said Capt. Scott Grabin. We walked in, introduced ourselves, and told him we were investigating the disappearance of a young boy, Dylan Weinberg.

"The kid's not here," said Grabin, going back to his paperwork.

"Maybe not," said Rambam. "But his nanny was shoved to her death off this platform today."

Grabin looked up. He thought for a moment, then put down his pen and leaned back in his chair.

"Okay," he said. "What can I do for you guys?"

"We know it's a long shot," said Rambam, "but we think the victim may have been involved with the boy's abduction. She may have been killed by someone who wanted to silence her or double-cross her."

"He seems to have succeeded on both counts," said Grabin dryly.

"We think that person knows what happened to the boy," said Rambam. "I know it's against the rules, but if you have any record of any eyewitnesses, we'd be very indebted to you."

Grabin looked at the two of us with inscrutable cop eyes. Then he sighed deeply and looked down at his desk for a moment. Then he glanced up again, a decision, apparently, having been made.

"Fuck the rules," he said. "Look at the piles of shit on this desk that probably nobody's ever going to see. Here. Take the file and go over to that empty desk. You've got five minutes. Then you're out of here and I never saw you guys."

We thanked Grabin, took the file, and went over to the desk with it. As you might expect, it was pretty slim pickings. In fact, we didn't even need our full five minutes. The file was only a few pages long and Rambam made chicken scratchings in his little private investigator's notebook, the kind a real crime buster carries, in which the pages flipped over the top. We thanked Grabin and handed him back the thin file; he said don't mention it. Then he said again, "I mean *really* don't mention it."

Back out on the platform, with trains roaring and clattering through the veins of the junkie that is New York, Rambam and I compared impressions of Grabin and the file. Rambam seemed almost wistful.

"He's a good cop," he said. "That's why he won't last long in the system. He shouldn't be stuck down here in the subway doing paperwork. He ought to be doing what we're doing."

"Right," I said. "Looking for lost boys and Peter Pan. What'd you make of the file?"

"Well, at least it's not the twelve blind men and the fucking elephant. I mean, there *does* appear to be something of a consensus."

"Of course, you have to consider the source. One of the eyewitnesses is a Nigerian selling wristwatches—"

"At least he should be accurate about the time."

"—another is a homeless man wearing a hat that, according to the file, sounds like it was stolen from the lead in a production of *The Pirates of Penzance.*"

"Just because they don't have homes," said Rambam, "doesn't mean they don't have eyes."

"The third eyewitness happens to be a defense lawyer. Nobody in their right mind's going to believe his bullshit."

"And the last eyewitness," finished Rambam, "seems to be some stock market genius who'll probably be jumping off the platform himself in a few months if the NASDAQ keeps plunging. That's about the right number of witnesses you'd expect in a situation like this. In fact, they're lucky to have gotten that many. More important, their descriptions of the killer are not wildly conflicting or incompatible with each other. The guy we're looking for carried a briefcase, wore a suit and tie, had a 'strange, desperate look in his eye,' and resembled a 'deranged businessman.' That ought to make it easy. There's only a few million guys like that running around Lower Manhattan."

"What do we do now, Mr. Hammett? I'm starting to feel like a canary in a coal mine down here."

"Cheer up. We're almost done. I can't believe they didn't interview the motorman on the train."

"Why's he so important?"

"He's the only guy in the place with a seat right on the fifty-yard line."

Rambam went looking for the motorman, and while he was at it, I went wandering around the platform, looking for the spot where it happened. There could be little forensic value in this activity, I decided. The cops and techs had already been there and gone. There would've been nothing left of Hattie anyway. Just a big, black, old lady from North Carolina who'd been waiting for a train back to Harlem that she was never going to make.

For something to do, I turned to a guy next to me and asked, "Was this where it happened?" He was a businessman in a suit and tie, carrying a briefcase. His eyes had a desperate, strange, deranged look. "Where what happened?" he asked. Then he looked at me suspiciously and moved a little farther down the platform.

About five minutes later, Rambam returned, rubbing his hands together like an insect. He even had a smile on his face.

"Same description we're working with," he said. "Only the motorman thinks our guy's a regular rider. He's definitely seen him before. We could try to catch the guy ourselves. That could mean, of course, hanging around a subway platform for the rest of our lives."

"Hey, everybody's got to be somewhere."

"Anyway, I think we have more immediate fish to fry. It's just possible we might make that trip up to Harlem tonight after all."

On the way upstairs, he took out his shoe phone and called Hattie's sister, whose name, I quickly learned, was Mattie. She, no doubt, was in a state of shock, but Rambam told her that only fast action now might catch the guy who did it, as well as helping to find the little boy whom Hattie had tended to for so many years. For all his aberrant social behavior and extra-legal activities, Rambam was not without charm. The sister agreed to see us as soon as we could get there.

"So it's Hattie told Mattie," I said, "just like the song."

"I sure as hell hope so," said Rambam, "because she isn't going to be telling anybody else."

TWENTY-NINE

A funny thing happened on the way to Harlem. We were stopped at a light at the corner of Fifth and Vermouth, when Rambam appeared to be taking an inordinate amount of interest in an old man closing up a newspaper stand. He stared at the old man as if he were a ghost from Yom Kippur past. He didn't notice that the lights had changed.

"It's code green, Kojak," I said.

"Thirty years ago," said Rambam, as he pulled away, "that would've been my great-grandfather. He was ninety-one when he died. I was ten. He left me one of those old-fashioned pill boxes. Inside it were all the ribbons and medals he'd received from the Union News Company. One of them was a length of service medal that read 70 YEARS. My mother told me they'd printed it especially for him. Nobody else before or since ever worked for the Union News Company for seventy years."

"Today the record would probably be about seventy minutes," I said.

"He used to eat liver and fried onions, which he cooked for himself every night. He'd also drink a glass of Napoleon Brandy. At ninety-one he fell and broke his hip. He had to close the news-stand, and they moved him into an old folks' home. Every night he'd cook fried liver and onions on a little hotplate in his room. And, of course, he'd always have a glass of Napoleon Brandy.

"Then the doctors and social workers came in and told him that liver and onions weren't good for him and they took away his hotplate. They also took away his Napoleon Brandy. He died two weeks later."

"When doctors and social workers get together," I said, "it's an especially deadly combination."

"Then you've got your grief counselors. What kid grows up wanting to be a grief counselor?"

"Could be why so many teenagers are croaking themselves these days. So they won't have to talk to grief counselors."

"And I'll bet nobody works at the same job for seventy years. Not too many even live that long."

"Maybe everybody should eat liver and fried onions cooked on a little hotplate every night. Accompanied, need I mention, by a glass of Napoleon Brandy."

"You forgot to include a side dish of guts, heart, and raw courage."

"We're not even in Harlem," said Rambam, "and we've already solved all the problems of the world."

"That's right," I said. "And we'll have fun, fun, fun 'til the social worker takes our hotplate away."

Rambam parked the car on 126th Street off Lenox Avenue and we walked the half block to Mattie Mamajello's apartment. The place resembled a graffiti graveyard. The stuff was everywhere you looked, on walls, on buildings, on curbsides, like cross ties on a railroad, like stars in the sky.

"Looks like a pretty solid 911 neighborhood," I said.

"Just keep walking," said Rambam.

There was a little over an hour until Cinderella time and the streets weren't crowded, but they weren't exactly empty either.

Painted women and winos and crackheads and dark denizens of the netherworld drifted by like ghosts in the night. Maybe they were just people like everybody else, but there was no time to stand around and find out. An argument was breaking out on the corner. A bottle was breaking. A heart was breaking in Harlem and nobody was thinking of staying around to pick up the pieces.

There was something oddly comforting about Rambam, a quality that reminded me a little of Tom Baker. Both the Baker-man and Rambam were big, tough guys, but they were also born or blessed with a measure of crazy that anybody could see from a mile away. This trait seemed to afford them a protection from Harlem and hells and winters in squalid apartments and fair-weather friends and love and loneliness and success and failure and even life and death for a while. Something burns in the eyes of that rare kind of person, like a match that kindles the flame. It burns bright in the darkest night and tells the world that it doesn't give a damn, friend.

Two painfully skinny female crackheads sat out on the stoop of Hattie's sister's building, barely acknowledging the two pale men walking through the nocturne of the neon night.

"We're here to see Mattie on the fifth floor," said Rambam.

"Buzzer's broken, door's open," one said. The other one seemed to be shivering from something colder than the cold.

Rambam pushed the door open and we walked into a shabby vestibule that smelled of whiskey and urine and cheap perfume and boasted almost as much graffiti as the street. There was a small elevator in the lobby, which we first thought we might take until we pushed the button and the doors opened to reveal a stark landscape of piss, puke, and shit, which even John Wayne would've been squeamish to ride through.

"We'll take the stairs," I said.

"That's an understatement," said Rambam.

Yet the stairway, too, seemed fraught with its own particular perils and unpleasantnesses. Each landing provided a new level of surprise and experience to our journey. One floor had large rats, another, used syringes, still another, two crazed crackheads hosing in the hallway. There was a body of a man lying comatose under a filthy blanket near one stairwell. There were holes in all the walls, more puddles of urine, and the capper was a screaming mimi who ran past us in the dark and a honey of a pile of detritus on the fifth floor stairwell indicating that a large mammal had passed this way recently.

We somehow found Mattie's door in the semi-gloom of the fifth-floor hallway, and we knocked. Mattie opened the door on a chain, studied us briefly, then closed the door, removed the chain, and welcomed us in to her apartment.

"It's a sad day," she said. "Hattie was my only sister. I guess the Lord must pick His most beautifulest flowers first."

"Yeah," said Rambam. "That's about par for the course."

"We're really sorry, Mattie," I added. "We're going to try very hard to catch this guy. We're also going to try very hard to find Dylan."

"Little Dylan," said Mattie. "Hattie's told me all about that boy."

Rambam was nodding and smiling behind her. She was a short, round, jolly-looking woman and she bore her grief bravely. She couldn't have known of Hattie's death for more than a number of hours, yet she was holding up admirably. For some reason, I thought of what the rabbi had told me at my mother's funeral: "I see it hasn't hit you yet." It had hit me, actually, and it got up my sleeve somewhat when he made the remark. We all grieve in our own personal way. Mostly, of course, we grieve for ourselves.

"You boys look like you could use a cup of coffee," she said, and she turned and led us through a clean, beautiful, well-kept apartment that was night and day to the rest of the building.

Soon we were all seated around a table in Mattie's kitchen, having three steaming cups of coffee and going through some old pictures of Hattie and Dylan on the farm upstate. Hattie was a short, wide-bodied woman much like her sister, with the same cheerful countenance about her whatever life put in her way.

"She loved those days on the farm with the boy," said Mattie. "Said they were some of the happiest times of her life. She'd been dreamin' of him a lot lately, she said. And when Hattie dreams, she dreams across time and place, and you come to find out it's always true."

I noticed Mattie slipping into the present tense when she spoke about her sister. Maybe it hadn't hit her yet.

"Did Hattie tell you any details about those dreams?" asked Rambam.

"She said Dylan was sad and lonely and he missed her. It made her terribly worried about him. He was in shnay—"

"There's the magic word again," said Rambam.

"—in a place with white light," she said. "And everybody was wearin' white robes."

"Sounds like heaven," I said. "Did Hattie dream that Dylan was in heaven?"

"Oh, Lordy, no!" said Mattie. "In the dreams he was very much alive here on earth. And what that woman dreams is always the God's truth. You can take my word for it. That boy's alive!"

"That's good to know," said Rambam, with a tone notably lacking in enthusiasm.

"By the way," I said, "where's this place upstate where the Weinbergs used to live?"

"Oh, I can't remember exactly what Hattie said. It was a small farm, though. Maybe twenty miles outside of Schenectady, New York. I couldn't tell you what direction 'cause I don't know."

"Mattie," I said. "You've been very helpful, especially under the circumstances. But this is very important. Did Hattie tell anybody besides you about these dreams?"

"Oh, didn't I mention it? That's where she was goin' this mornin'. To tell Mr. Weinberg."

THIRTY

It was later that night, after Rambam had dropped me off at the Monkey's Paw, that I finally had a chance to sip a few pints of Guinness and sift through my own recent experiences traveling down the winding, muddy river of life. The two investigations, almost tangentially, seemed to be coming to a head nearly as deep and satisfying as the one on my Guinness. But this was precisely the time in any case when pilot error could prove fatal. At the dawn of discovery, there is the human tendency for any detective to want to try to speed things along to their natural conclusion. But right now, at the weary tail end of a slow Monday night at the bar, this was the time to follow the great Davy Crockett's advice: "Be sure you're right, then go ahead." Davy, one of the heroes of the Alamo, had died with a garland of dead Mexicans all around him.

But a true mender of destinies, as I aspired to be, must go beyond merely being morally or intellectually right. He must demonstrate why he's right. He must show how he got there. In other words, it's fine to be right, but now you have to prove it. In the immortal words of Johnny Cochran, that great African-American seeker of truth and justice: "If the glove don't fit, you must acquit."

You could stitch that one on a pillow in hell, I thought, as I ordered another Guinness. By this time, cats with three legs and little autistic children were walking the criss-crossed country roads of my imagination and populating the hotels of my dreams. My dreams, unfortunately, were not as encouraging as Hattie's. I saw dark images of the body of a little boy being buried in rich, fertile soil. I saw the dark form of a man with a spade in his hand. He was wearing a dark overcoat and a pair of black gloves. The gloves fit perfectly.

Somewhere midway through my third Guinness I remembered a story I'd read fairly recently. A Swiss guy had written a book about his experiences as a child survivor of a Nazi concentration camp. Though his accounts appeared to be impeccably accurate, the books were later pulled from the shelves when the man turned out to be a fraud. No one knows why a person would want to fabricate his involvement in such a horrific experience, but there're lots of sick fucks out there and, just like everyone else, they need hobbies.

The salient point, however, was the way this guy was finally exposed. An Israeli journalist, after interviewing the man, was the first to suspect him of being a fraud. From there, more investigation was done, and the man's house of cards began to tumble. This journalist had previously interviewed scores of concentration camp survivors, including members of his own family, and he noted an interesting distinction between this would-be survivor and the real ones. The Israeli said that throughout the interview the man was weeping, wiping away tears with a handkerchief. In all his past experience with concentration camp survivors, he'd never seen one of them shed a tear. They described their hellish personal nightmares dry-eyed, every one of them. There were no more tears left to shed, possibly. Or, perhaps, their eyes no longer truly trusted people. Anne Frank wrote in her diary that she still believed "in the goodness of man." She was an exceptional girl and I felt sorry she couldn't've lived to hang out with me or Davy Crockett or even an investment banker with a three-inch dick. But had she survived and talked about her experiences, I don't believe she would've cried.

But Vic Weinberg had cried. He'd wept all through my first interview with him. Not his wife. Not Julia. Only Vic. Maybe it hadn't meant anything. Maybe it was just the Guinness thinking for me. I myself cried at movies and weddings almost ritually. But I hadn't cried at my mother's funeral. Either it hadn't hit me yet or it'd hit me a long, long time ago.

We'd already planned to interview Weinberg the following day, but we'd have to be very careful. Just because he was a crybaby and Hattie had told him of her dream prophesies did not make him guilty of killing his own son. But add to that the scenario of the deranged businessman inexplicably killing an old black nanny at a subway stop just a few blocks from his office, and Weinberg was starting to look better and better. Then, in good Miss Marple fashion, I thought of the family that we'd known in the fifties where the kid had a host of physical and emotional problems, and when he was about fifteen years old he'd gotten into the millionth argument with his father and his father had killed him. Maybe Weinberg hadn't wanted to wait that long.

But all of this speculation was based on the flimsiest of psychological and circumstantial evidence, I realized. There'd been no ransom demand. There'd been no trail of the kidnapping. There'd been no nothing. There were only two ways this one was going to get solved: if Weinberg confessed, or if we turned up the body. Neither seemed very likely at the moment. At the moment, all we had were Hattie's dreams.

THIRTY-ONE

ic Weinberg's office building was so close to the subway station I could feel it rumbling in my stomach as I stood in the hallway outside his office. It was Tuesday morning, around 10:45. Rambam, in his suit and tie, could've passed for a Wall Street executive coming in a little late for work. I, on the other hand, could've passed for a homeless person who'd wandered from the subway platform.

"So you think he planted the kid down on the farm?" said Rambam.

"I think it's the logical place."

"They buried Jimmy Hoffa in a logical place and no one's found him since."

"But those guys were pros. This guy's a wimpy little Wall Street Jew. He might've not even meant to croak the kid. He's an amateur. It could've been an accident."

"Like the accident that happened at the subway station yesterday afternoon?"

"Good point."

"Look," I said. "We've got to do this carefully. You handled the thing with Mattie, let me take the lead here. I've already got something of a rapport with Vic."

"I'd trade a Vic for a Mattie any day."

"The other thing is I just don't want to create a stink in here."

"Creating a stink is my middle name," said Rambam.

"That's another reason for me to handle the negotiations," I said.

Weinberg's secretary was not overjoyed that we were there without an appointment. I told her my name and that Vic would be happy to see me. I may have exaggerated a little, but, with only about a ten-minute wait, Rambam and I were escorted into his office.

It wasn't exactly a cubicle, but it definitely wasn't the corner office. Vic looked like half the man I'd seen two weeks ago and he hadn't looked all that good then. He was gaunt and haggard and seemed to have developed a bothersome little tic around his right eye. I introduced him to Rambam, whom I said was my associate. Rambam did not look too pleased with the new job title, but at least he didn't throw Weinberg's ficus plant against the wall.

"Any news on Dylan?" Weinberg wanted to know.

"I'm afraid not," I said.

"I guess it was too much to hope for," he mumbled distract-edly.

"I guess you read about what happened to Hattie Mamajello the other day?" I said.

"Terrible," he said. "Terrible."

There was a brief pause in the action. I wanted to give him enough rope to get his foot caught by Moby Dick's harpoon line. But Weinberg had a line of his own and it almost worked.

"She was up here to see me that morning, you know."

I did, but I feigned ignorance. The way things were going with this case, it wasn't difficult.

"She'd been living in North Carolina since we let her go. Didn't even know Dylan was missing. She always got along with me better than Sylvia, so she just came up here, looking to get her job back. It wasn't easy telling her about Dylan and I'm afraid she took it very hard."

Here was a lie for sure, but he was doing so well I just let him keep going. He changed the subject quickly and began whining about his financial troubles having been compounded recently by his troubles with the farm.

"I'm sorry," he said, "but I thought I'd unloaded this farm we had, but now, on top of everything else, it looks like the deal's fallen through. Now the attorney says there'll have to be a foreclosure on the people we sold it to and the thing comes right back to me again like the proverbial albatross—"

"Bottle imp," I said.

"Whatever," said Vic Weinberg.

It seemed like he might have run out of material, and Rambam had gotten up and was pacing around the little office like a wind-up toy, but I wasn't quite through with Weinberg yet.

"Where is this farm, Mr. Weinberg?" I asked.

"Upstate New York," he said matter-of-factly.

"Near Schenectady, right?"

It was quick as a flash. In fact, it was a flash of something like curiosity, or calculation, or doubt in the troubled eyes of Vic Weinberg. It was over in a flash, too, but I'd seen it and so had Rambam.

"That's right," he said. "Now if you guys don't have anything else, I've got to get back to work."

We shook hands with Weinberg like two football captains before a big game and then we left. It was a big game, all right. Everything was a big game.

"Why don't we take your borrowed Lincoln up to Schenectady?" I said to Rambam as we exited the building.

"Fine with me," he said. "I've just got to pick up my toilet kit and a shovel."

"We might as well take our time, have a nice drive through the countryside. It's north of here, isn't it?"

"Everything's north from New York City," said Rambam. "Except Texas."

"Ever been to Schenectady?"

"Sure. Millions of times. Haven't you?"

"I can't remember if I ever made a trip there or not."

"I don't think you're going to forget this one," said Rambam.

THIRTY-TWO

If you've ever thought about driving from New York City to Schenectady, think again. The drive seems interminable. If your driving companion is Rambam, the conversation may become a little overheated at times, but that's not entirely bad because otherwise you may freeze your balls off. As we left the friendly confines of Manhattan very late that night, we'd both come to the conclusion that there was a high probability Weinberg had "planted the kid down on the farm," to borrow an especially sensitive phrase from Rambam.

"But do you think he'd have brought up the farm in the first place," I asked, "if he'd buried the boy there?"

"Of course," said Rambam. "The guy's a Wall Street weasel. It's just a dodge to throw us off in case we were thinking that way. I see fucking guys like him every day. You can't believe a fucking word they tell you."

"You're kidding? I thought Vic was a pretty nice guy."

"Mr. Congeniality," said Rambam. "Right up there with the Boston Strangler and Ted Bundy. He gets my vote for most likely to push an old nanny from a subway platform. When we get back, I'll show his pic to the motorman and ten-to-one we'll have an eyewitness identification."

"But still no hard evidence."

"Which is why we're reenacting *The Bobbsey Twins Go to the Farm*."

"I just hope Hattie was right. That the kid's still alive."

"After all this time? That's just wishful thinking."

"Maybe that's what all dreams are."

And so I fell into somewhat of a dream state myself, passing highways and lights and rivers and bridges and towns full of people who slept in their beds. There is something about traveling across the countryside in a car or a train or a bus that stirs the rhythm and the flow of the imagination, shaking loose thoughts and pictures and notions into that swagman's bag filled with the stuff of dreams come true.

As I traveled through the night, gliding gently in and out of sleep, as so often happens, my thoughts were not on where I was or where I was going, but far away, just outside of Utopia, Texas. I saw Nancy Niland, whom I only knew as a generous benefactor of the Rescue Ranch and a voice on the phone, getting out of her dark-colored van with a bag full of gifts for the dogs. I saw her leave when she discovered Cousin Nancy and Tony weren't home. I watched her come back a few hours later in the same van and learn that Lucky was gone and help Nancy and Tony look for him in vain. And all the while she was fighting her own brave battle that no one could help her with.

That, of course, was not what Josephine had thought she'd seen. She'd seen a man get out the first time, then a few hours later, the same van comes back and a woman gets out. But in my mind I saw Nancy Niland getting out both times. Then I saw Cousin Nancy, a heart as big as Texas, absentminded sometimes, pushed to paranoia by Art Bell's talk of UFOs and satanic cults and the petty harassment of some of her small-town neighbors. I saw two wolves howling at something that wasn't the moon. I saw Lucky, somewhere out in the surrounding countryside, weaving his wondrous way back to the Rescue Ranch. I didn't know if he was going to make it. I wasn't sure if any of us would.

Early that morning, when we pulled into a roadside diner, I went to a pay phone and called two women who both were named Nancy and who both lived in Texas. I verified my new version of the events with the first one, then I wished her good luck. I told the second one to expect a little bit of luck to be coming her way soon, too.

THIRTY-THREE

chenectady's a town of about 65,000 people and most of them seemed to be milling around in the County Government Office Building. After wandering about aimlessly, we were finally directed to the tax assessor's office by an old man in a sweatshirt that read: I'M SHY BUT I HAVE A BIG DICK. The woman at the tax assessor's office directed us to the public access terminal of a computer at which Rambam immediately sat down and started computing. After futzing with the machine for a while, he turned to me with a look of frustration.

"Weinberg's not even listed," he said.

"Remember," I said, "the place is in some kind of foreclosure. Can you go back a few years?"

"I wish to hell I could," he said.

"Why? I thought things were going well with Julia."

"They are. But when things seem to be going this well something bad always happens."

"I hate to say this, but that's a very Jewish attitude."

"Thanks for the help, rabbi. Now if you'll shut the fuck up for a minute I'll try to get this information for us."

I wandered around the tax assessor's office for a while, looking at framed Norman Rockwell paintings. There was nothing really wrong with Norman Rockwell, I thought. The only thing that kept him from greatness was too much irritating gentile optimism. At last Rambam found a block and lot number belonging to the Weinbergs and brought it back to the same lady who directed him to a large drawing table full of tax maps of every conceivable kind. This nuts-and-bolts aspect of detective work always seemed to fascinate Rambam but always managed to bore me into leaving the cocktail party early. Now he was skipping through the tax maps with the fanatic eagerness of a pervert at a porno site.

Eventually, we had what we needed, got out of the building, back in the Lincoln, and soon we were on our merry way to the wonderful Weinberg family farm. A front had come in and the weather was cold and gray and grim, perfect atmosphere for grave digging.

"I've been thinking," I said, as we turned on to a small farm road, "that twenty acres is a pretty small spread by Texas standards, but it could prove to be a hell of a lot for the two of us to cover."

"That's right, pal," said Rambam. "The good news is that the ground around here seems pretty hard and flat, and it shouldn't be all that difficult to find the freshly dug, shallow grave of a child. Also, a lot of Weinberg's land seems to run along the road. I think we can rule those easily accessible sections out. But the truth is, even methane gas detectors wouldn't help us that much. What we really need are dogs and men. If we'd had any hard evidence, we could've gone to the local sheriff or the police. This is a different world up here from New York City. I doubt if they've even heard about the case up here. We couldn't exactly tell them we need their help because we're on a mission from God following the dreams of a dead black nanny named Hattie Mamajello. Now where the hell's Farm Road 2352?"

"Don't lay this on Hattie. She thought the boy was still alive."

"And I think we'll find she was probably wrong," said Rambam, as he hooked a vicious right onto Farm Road 2352, flinging gravel all the way to Albany.

"Or we may find nothing at all."

"Maybe you could get on the batphone and call Cousin Nancy and have her send up some of her four-legged friends. We could recruit local men from the area. Did you always want to be a detective when you grew up? Now's your chance for on-the-job training! We could give each man a dog and a shovel, and pretty soon they'd all be fighting and biting and sucking and fucking each other, and the place would look like a fucking prairie dog colony—"

"—or the dark side of Uranus—"

"No, that's wrong. The men wouldn't show up for the job. Nobody'd come out to help find a missing little autistic boy from New York City. Now if we told them that Pinhead the Pirate buried his legendary treasure here—"

"My, aren't we cynical. I hate to tell you this, but that's a very Jewish attitude."

"Rabbi," said Rambam, as he pulled up to the farm. "Fuck yourself."

Whoever Weinberg had sold the place to obviously hadn't been much of a hand at farming. The place looked dilapidated and forlorn and right out of central casting for burying a body. The barn was falling down and the house looked like Boo Radley lived there. Weeds had grown up everywhere. There was no sign that anyone had been there in many months. Actually, there was a sign, but it read: FORECLOSURE.

"Well, at least Weinberg was telling the truth about one thing," said Rambam. "The farm is certainly in foreclosure."

"Yeah," I said. "And it looks like the last occupants were Wavy Gravy and the Hog Farm Commune."

"Or the Manson family," said Rambam.

For two investigators to search even a farm as small as twenty acres would require much more time than we were willing to give to the project. It didn't take us long to see that there was no evidence of freshly disturbed soil, but our methodology, admittedly, was unscientific and, as a result, unprofitable. For the better part of several hours we split up and searched the barren fields of the property, to no avail. We pored carefully over copses of trees, overgrown gardens, and the areas around and behind the structures on the place. Lastly, we went through the house and the barn together.

"It sounded like a good idea at the time," said Rambam, poking through what used to be a kitchen for any signs of recent habitation. There were none.

"It doesn't mean he's not buried here," I said.

"Or that Weinberg didn't kill the kid and just throw him in the river."

"That's possible, but there's no sign of anybody being on the property for a long time. Not even neighborhood vandals."

"No dogs, no men, no grave," said Rambam. "The farm may be a nonstarter."

We were walking toward the barn when we heard a strange, strangled-sounding noise from inside the closed wooden doors. Rambam took out a gun and we both walked gingerly toward the barn doors. We stopped and listened again. Once more we heard the sound, a little louder this time. It was almost familiar, yet unidentifiable—like somebody trying to scream through a gag.

"I'll go in first," said Rambam.

"When Cleve is carrying my guitar on a gig he always wants me to go first. He says: 'Star before guitar.' "

"Well, in this case," said Rambam, "it's Glock before schmuck."

Then Rambam unhitched the unlocked door and pulled it open. If it was gray outside, it was black inside the barn. Rambam took a small flashlight out of his coat and began to shine it into the darkness. Moats of dust danced crazily in the beam. Then toward the back of the barn, behind a huge pile of hay, we heard the sound again.

"What the fuck?" muttered Rambam, rushing ahead with the light and leaving me alone in the semidarkness.

"Unpleasant," I said to the bats who'd begun flying wildly about the barn.

Rambam had now skirted the haystack and had totally disappeared from my line of vision. I edged forward slowly, like a man in a dream. Before I even got to the haystack I heard Rambam's voice echoing loudly through the dark, dank barn.

"Jesus Christ!" he shouted.

"Is it the kid?" I said.

"No," said Rambam. "It's the skinniest fucking rooster I've ever seen in my entire fucking life!"

THIRTY-FOUR

T
he drive back to Schenectady, to use the much-loved convention of a sport analogy, was like the plane ride back home for the team that just lost the big game. The weather was depressing. The scenery was depressing. The situation was depressing. We'd liberated the pathetic, near-dead rooster from the large wire enclosure and, undoubtedly, saved his life. If Buddha had been watching, we certainly had scored some points for the coming final exam. That, however, was hardly the reason we'd come to the farm.

Just to fill the spiritual void we both felt at the moment, I recounted to Rambam a story, as I remembered it, by the great Texas author, folklorist, and naturalist J. Frank Dobie. In the tale, Dobie tells of his experience in the early fifties traveling through the backroads of Oklahoma and coming upon a run-down, old-fashioned trading post.

Walking around the side of the place, he saw a small, rusty cage, maybe two feet by two feet. Inside the cage, where it could not quite even stretch its wings, was a golden eagle that had recently been captured and was being sold into captivity. He noticed that the beautiful bird's head was bloodied from trying to break its way out of the cage. He also noticed that the cage was not locked. It was secured by a hasp and a rusty piece of wire. The thought came into Dobie's mind that it would not take him long to twist the wire, open the hasp, and release the eagle back into the wild.

There was a moment when he could've done just that. But he didn't.

By the time he'd thought about it, hesitated, then thought about it again and decided upon taking action, a tough-looking man came out of the store, as if suspecting his intentions, and said, "Two hundred bucks, friend, and the bird is yours." Dobie at that time had nothing like two hundred dollars to his name. The man watched him carefully as he went back to his car and drove away.

He wasn't able to return to Oklahoma and that trading post for another six months, by which time the golden eagle and the cage were gone, possibly sold to a zoo or bought by a wealthy customer. But the eagle, Dobie knew in his heart, was never returned to the wild where he belonged.

He came back one more time, years later, only to find that the whole trading post was gone, a victim of the new superhighway that did not stop there. But from the incident, Dobie knew that he would never regret the things he had done; he'd only regret the things he hadn't. And he also knew that golden eagle would stay with him for the rest of his life.

It was a story that I'd read in college and never forgotten, and that, in some not unimportant ways, had probably changed my life. I wasn't even sure that Rambam had been listening, but apparently he had, because now he spoke up.

"J. Frank Dobie finds a golden eagle and all we find is a scrawny rooster," he said.

"You've got to factor in inflation," I said. "You can't expect as much for your dollar these days."

"I expected more than we got," said Rambam. "Other than liberating one anorexic rooster, we didn't accomplish a fucking thing on this trip."

I couldn't disagree with him. The only solace I took was in the fact that detective work in some ways is very similar to science. The things you don't discover may be just as important as the things you do discover, because they help to narrow the beam of light you hope someday to shine upon the truth. As in science, "someday" in detective work is never soon enough, especially when lives may be at stake. Yet for a true mender of destiny, failure and success are both impostors; they are only significant if they provide the brick and mortar for the road that leads to how things came to be.

"Maybe Hattie was right," I said. "Vic Weinberg's a Jew and there ain't many of them on death row. Maybe he didn't kill his son."

"I don't know," said Rambam. "I just know the number of Jews on death row is going to increase by one very soon, because he *did* kill Hattie. The motorman on the subway will confirm that as soon as we get back to the city and I get my hands on a pic of Vic."

"But where's the kid?" I said, as the trees and cars and rivers moved by uncaring in the cold, gray afternoon. "Where's the kid?"

THIRTY-FIVE

I t was just on the outskirts of town when I saw the sign. It was an old faded billboard by the highway that obviously had seen a lifetime of snow and rain and sleet and sludge, not to mention the occasional bullet holes and assorted decorative efforts from the southern end of birds heading north. The sign was meant to read: THE CHURCH OF CHRIST WELCOMES YOU TO SCHENECTADY. JESUS IS OUR QUARTERBACK. Unfortunately, or fortunately, depending on how you looked at it, the hands of time and the previously mentioned effluvia had managed to desecrate some of the original wording. Indeed, the middle part of the word "Schenectady" had been almost totally obscured.

When it hit me, it landed like a ton of bricks. At first, I didn't know what it meant, but then my weatherbeaten brain, subconsciously perhaps, picked up the bricks and, moving with the speed of light and love and madness, constructed a road to the truth. It had to be, I thought. It just *had* to be.

"That sign!" I shouted. "Look at that sign!"

"Yeah?" said Rambam casually. "If Jesus is our quarterback, I guess we're not going to the Super Bowl this year."

"But don't you see it? It's shnay!"

"Shnay? What the fuck is shnay? It's just a nonsense word this kid used to irritate people. And right now it's irritating me."

"Don't you see? Vic Weinberg *had* to kill Hattie. She was the only one who knew the boy was in shnay."

"What do you mean *in* shnay?"

"In Hattie's dream, according to her sister, the boy was in shnay."

"How can you be in shnay?"

"Easy. You're on the outskirts of it right now."

"*Schenectady?*" Rambam stared at me a little longer than was prudent for a man driving a vehicle faster than God makes Wal-Mart stores.

"Imagine if you were a three- or four-year-old child trying to pronounce the word 'Schenectady.' Especially if you're mimicking a nanny with a heavy southern accent. And if, on top of that, you're emotionally disturbed, or communicationally impaired or—"

"As we shrinks like to say: 'Fucked up.' "

"—and being autistic, both the word and the world closes down. Instead of mispronouncing the word 'spaghetti' like many little kids do, and then learning later the correct pronunciation, with a special kid like this the pronunciation stays the same. And there's probably another reason the word stayed with Dylan and never changed. It connotes warmth and comfort and, sad to say for a young child, happier times. It means 'home.' "

"So you think Vic dumped the kid somewhere in Schenectady?"

"Hattie's dream ices it. I think Weinberg used the foreclosure of the farm as an excuse, if he ever needed one, to be up here. I think he suckered the kid along with the promises of going home."

"The kid's pretty screwed up. He couldn't just have dumped him at the general hospital. It's got to be some out-of-the-way, extended care place for children. Maybe an orphan's home of some kind. If you're right."

"I'm not right. Hattie's right. And I think we should go right to the police."

"We don't need the police," said Rambam. "We need the fire department."

Now it was my turn to wonder whether Rambam was cookin' on another planet. I didn't have to wait long to realize that, in most respects, he was still in somewhat tenuous touch with the mothership.

"The cops won't be any good at this," he said. "The only ones who know where everything is in a town are the guys at the local fire station. If a guy reports a fire from Bob's Deli and Gun Shop, for instance, and the connection breaks off, they already know exactly where it is. All we've got to do is tell them what we're looking for."

"Smells good from here."

"First, of course, we've got to find the local fire station."

This proved a little more difficult than it should have because the first guy we asked gave us a particularly hideous set of directions. After that, we stopped at a tackle-and-bait shop and the guy simply gestured down the street and there it was.

"Doesn't seem like a lot of activity," I said, as we pulled into the parking lot of the little firehouse.

"There never is," said Rambam, "unless there's a fire. Then, the place suddenly becomes Grand Central Station."

At the moment, the place looked more like Sleepy Hollow. A large brown dog was sleeping on the floor. Two men were playing a game of chess that seemed almost as lethargic as the dog. They did not look up as Rambam and I walked into the fire station.

Rambam and I crossed over to the men and still we got no reaction. My sidekick turned to me. "Your move," he said.

"Excuse me, gentlemen," I said. "We're private investigators from the city trying to find a missing child." Rambam looked at me dubiously. The two firemen looked up slowly, as if cobwebs were attached to their heads and they didn't want to break them.

"If a father were trying to dump a kid at some low-profile orphanage-type setup in this area, where would he take him?"

The two men glanced at each other. Neither said a word. Finally, one of them spoke.

"You say you're from the city?" he said. "Schenectady?"

"The other city," said Rambam. "New York."

"You guys for real?" said the second fireman.

"No," said Rambam. "We're two Russian chess masters who just happened to be passing by and we thought we'd check the competition. Get it?"

I could tell that Rambam, though still highly witty, was rapidly running out of charm. It was his idea to go to the fire station, and so far it certainly wasn't succeeding as planned.

"Of *course* we're for real," said Rambam, in a voice of such urgency and potential malice that it woke up the dog. "Now are you guys going to fucking *help* us or *not?*"

"Try Swafford's Orphan and Foundling Home," said the first fireman. "It's the only place like that around here. An old man, Lamoine Swafford, has run the place forever. Take a left at the light and go about four miles."

"Thanks," said Rambam, as we headed out of the little station. "By the way, your rook's in danger."

THIRTY-SIX

S wafford's Orphan and Foundling Home looked like something out of a lesser Charles Dickens novel. In the lengthening shadows of the chilly, leaden afternoon, it looked about as old as God and, quite possibly, just as vengeful. It was a long, low rambling, nondescript structure with gray smoke escaping from a small chimney to join the gray clouds. You got the feeling they were cooking porridge.

"Kind of redundant, isn't it?" said Rambam. "Orphan and Foundling Home."

"Not to mention alarmingly politically incorrect," I said. "It could be run by the same people who helped your great-grandfather by taking away the liver and onions and the little hotplate."

"Don't forget the Napoleon Brandy."

We pulled into the almost-empty gravel parking lot and surveyed the depressing-looking structure. We briefly discussed our strategy for when we got inside the place.

"Judging from your performance at the fire station," I said, "maybe I should open diplomatic relations with Lamoine Swafford."

"You want to be Neville Chamberlain," said Rambam congenially, "you go right ahead."

"I don't want to be Neville Chamberlain. I just don't want you to knock the man's hearing aid down his throat and then we find out the kid's not there."

"How about if I just knock that cigar down *your* throat?"

"It'd probably lodge there and I'd choke to death."

"Good. At least you'd finally stop smoking."

"I just hope you're prepared for McGovern's headline in the *Daily News:* COUNTRY LEGEND KILLED BY LOCAL MAN."

"Yeah, but the *Post* would probably take a different slant: FAMOUS PRIVATE INVESTIGATOR SLAYS OVER-THE-HILL MUSICIAN."

"And the *Times* would take a still different approach," I said. "MORE EVIDENCE THAT CIGARS ARE HARMFUL."

"Let's get the fucking kid," said Rambam. "*If* he's here."

We got out of the Lincoln and headed up the winding walkway to the place. I steeled myself for the same feeling I always got whenever I visited a local dog pound. Even before you open the door, the very walls seem to scream inside your head: "Take *me!*" Upon reflection, however, I do recall as we walked up that ill-kept pathway, a strong sense of something that I'd have to call destiny. And if there's one thing I know about destiny it is that you can't count on it forever.

A burly woman in a white nurse's uniform greeted us first and took us to a rather sad-looking visitors' waiting room. It looked like it'd been waiting for visitors for a very long time. The nurse said she'd get Mr. Swafford for us. Rambam sat down on a folding chair and picked up a decidedly ancient issue of *Boy's Life.*

"You might learn something from that," I said.

"Yeah," said Rambam. "How to stay out of places like this."

I got up and paced the little waiting room. Places like this couldn't help being places like this, I thought. It felt a little like a home, a little like a hospital, a little like a prison. If you stayed in a place like this for more than a few years, I felt, it would serve to wrap your soul in an institutional gauze that would stay with you forever. You would always be a bit like a child dressing up in adult clothes, play-acting in the attic, no matter how old you were. For a kid like Dylan, no one could predict what effect institutionalization might have upon him. He might come out of his shell or withdraw even further into it. Possibly, it would have no effect at all, since he was born with that layer of gauze between himself and the world.

Lamoine Swafford came into the room and shook hands with both of us and asked how he could help us. He was dressed in a white suit that might've looked resplendent decades ago. A man in his mid to late seventies, he had about him something of the aura of a kindly shepherd amongst his flock. He reported that he had no record of a Dylan Weinberg, or of a Victor Weinberg.

"That's not terribly surprising," said Rambam. "Any parent who's planning to abandon his own child is probably not going to do it using their real names."

"My mother did," said Swafford. "She left me at a little place like this in Albany when I was four years old. She kissed me goodbye and promised she'd come back for me when she could."

"Did she ever come back?" I asked.

"Not yet," said Lamoine Swafford.

We showed Swafford the photo of Dylan Weinberg and asked if he recognized the boy. He put on a thick pair of glasses and studied it for a few moments. He said he didn't think so.

"At this moment," he said, "we house over a hundred and fifty boys and girls here. The little toddlers have a chance maybe. The older kids will probably be with us until they reach legal adulthood. It's very sad really, but nobody usually wants to adopt the older kids."

"How old are what you consider to be the older kids?" Rambam asked.

Lamoine Swafford thought about it a moment. Then he took off his glasses, folded them, and put them in the pocket of his coat.

"Over six," he said.

Swafford took us on tour of the place, with special attention to boys in Dylan's age range. Sadly, there didn't seem to be any other visitors. Yet, even as the ubiquitous institutional gauze was forming over some of the children's eyes, others appeared bright-eyed, cheerful, almost carefree. My mind unbiddingly drifted back to the Rescue Ranch, that "happy orphanage" for stray dogs, far away in Utopia. The eyes of the dogs and the eyes of the kids were unnervingly identical in this respect: Each individual pair of eyes peered into your soul and silently, longingly, told you that all they wanted in the world was a home.

As the tour was coming to its conclusion, Rambam made a final pitch to Lamoine Swafford. It seemed to me like he was flailing the passive horse of Judaism, but I suppose I couldn't fault him for trying.

"The kid we're looking for has special problems," said Rambam. "He may say nothing or seem very shy. But he's about ten years old and would've been brought in a little over two weeks ago. And he may not look like his photograph."

"Wait a minute," said Swafford. "There was a child brought in fairly recently who was about ten and had leukemia. He'd been through chemotherapy and had lost all his hair. He was moved to the hospital unit."

"Where's the hospital unit?" I asked, holding my breath.

"Right this way."

We followed Swafford down the hallway and off to a wing on the right. We stood in a doorway and peered around the corner at ten little patients in ten little beds on the far side of the hospital unit.

"It's not state of the art," said Swafford, "but we have a doctor on call and a home nursing staff that checks on us daily. Some of the nurses are here now, along with a few of our own staff."

The room appeared to be filled with a bright white light from the fluorescent fixtures along the ceiling. The nurses and the orphanage staff were all dressed in white uniforms. There was a small boy with almost no hair on his head in the last bed from the door. Swafford did not appear eager for us to enter the unit, and I couldn't quite see what the boy was doing.

"The boy without the hair," I said. "Is he doing a puzzle or something?"

"He's building a model airplane," said Swafford. "You know, he's pretty good."

Moments later, Lamoine Swafford, Rambam, and I stood by the foot of the little hospital bed. The boy appeared to be totally engrossed in building his model airplane.

"Dylan?" I said.

He looked up from the little airplane. He favored the three of us with a beautiful smile.

"Shnay," he said.

"Jesus," I whispered to Rambam. "I just wish Hattie could've been around."

"Who do you think led us here?" he said.

THIRTY-SEVEN

It was way past Cinderella time when Rambam dropped me off at the loft. I fed the cat, smiled back at the puppet-head, and poured the very last of the Jameson's directly down my neck from the bottle, thereby saving unneeded wear and tear on the old bull's horn. My head was halfway to the pillow when the phones rang. I made the forced march through a darkened Europe in my purple sarong and finally reached the desk and collared the blower on the left.

"Start talkin'," I said.

It was Cousin Nancy. In all the time I'd known her, she had almost never engendered nor received a telephone call after 8:00 P.M. Through the process of deductive reasoning I concluded that this had to be either very good news or very bad news.

"Kinky!" she said, in the out-of-breath voice of an excited child. "Guess what?"

"Lucky's back," I said.

"How did you know?"

"I took an educated stab in the dark."

"But you sort of told me yesterday he'd be coming back soon. How'd you know that?"

I lit a half-smoked cigar and turned on the lamp on the desk.

Now we'd reached the point where even the great Sherlock Holmes knew he had to be particularly careful. If you refused to divulge your methods, the client would think you'd merely gotten lucky, no pun intended. If you explained thoroughly how you came to your conclusions, the client would then realize that greatest of all crime-solving secrets, that the best detective work is really child's play. In other words, you were screwed either way. It was the catch-22 that drove Sherlock Holmes to cocaine.

"I had my own theory for where Lucky was, but I was troubled by Josephine's eyewitness account of the identical van arriving twice that night, the first time being driven by a man and the second time by a woman whom we identified as Nancy Niland. But Nancy Niland was fighting cancer at the time and, I later verified, going through chemotherapy. So the first visitor Josephine saw was Nancy with extremely short hair. The second visitor was Nancy wearing a wig. The bag she was carrying was full of dog treats."

"That's amazing," said Cousin Nancy. "But then where *was* Lucky?"

"We're all a bit forgetful at times, Nancy, especially when our minds are on something else. You forgot to bring me the Hill's Science Diet cat food several times. I forgot to call my brother Roger in Maryland. But, to answer your question, you locked the trailer that night but you forgot to close the back window after you finished smudging the place. Lucky jumped out into the darkness and became a stowaway in the back of your truck.

"I've done some research on wolves and they know their friends well, of which you were one. The only time they invariably howl is at exactly an hour before dawn. The reason they howled that night when you arrived to feed them was because something was different and something was wrong. That something was Lucky in the back of the truck."

"Poor Lucky."

"That was his reaction, too. He jumped out when you were feeding the wolves and ran for the hills. He'd never heard wolves howling before and he wanted to put as much distance between them and himself as possible. Incidentally, on the subject of wolves again, they are—different in some rather interesting ways from dogs. If you teach one dog how to open a rather complicated gate at the Rescue Ranch, all the others can watch him do it every day and not be able to do it themselves. If you teach one wolf how to open that gate, every wolf in the pack picks up the trick instantaneously. The only thing no one's ever been able to train a wolf to do, by the way, is to sit."

"But the wolves are almost twenty miles away," said Nancy. "How did Lucky ever find his way back?"

"That," I said, "is a question for a higher authority."

It was rather amazing now that I thought about it. A cat with only three legs and a little boy who on most occasions only speaks the word "shnay" are both missing, and both found on the very same day. It was as if unbeknownst to the rest of the world, defying every law of science and man, they were somehow in touch with each other. It was, I reflected, almost enough to make you believe in God or at least astrology.

"Okay, Nancy," I said. "Give Lucky a welcome home hug for me."

"I already have," said Nancy.

"And be sure to tell Magoo I love him."

"He knows it," she said.

WEINBERG FAMILY EPILOGUE

The Weinberg Family, like many other families in the world, could not remain forever in the idyllic state of how-it-used-to-be back on the farm. Like *Bob Dylan's Dream,* the roads they traveled had shattered and split. It was a little thing called growing up. It was a little thing called life.

Dylan Weinberg was bound over to the proper authorities by Lamoine Swafford and soon returned to the custody of his mother, Sylvia. The latest report is that he is doing well and said to be "normalizing," for want of a better word.

Victor Weinberg, of course, is a different story. To quote Rambam: "His sell-by date had been reached." The day after Dylan was located in Schenectady, Weinberg was arrested by my old friends Detective Sergeants Cooperman and Fox. He was initially charged with child abandonment, filing a false police report on a missing child, and being an asshole, which, as Rambam also pointed out, "is only a misdemeanor charge in New York."

While holding him in custody, Cooperman and Fox got a court order for a line-up, and the subway motorman I.D.'d Weinberg, thereby nailing him on the murder charge for the death of Hattie Mamajello. Weinberg will soon go to trial where he could receive the death penalty, or life in prison, or, if he's lucky, wind up with merely a long prison term from which he emerges with an ass-hole the size of a walnut.

Julia Weinberg and Rambam went through a rather sudden estrangement after her father's arrest. I assume, quite naturally, that she was in an understandable snit because of the crucial hand Rambam had played in tossing her dad in the sneezer. Just last week I saw her coming up Vandam Street toward the loft. I said hello, but she walked right by and didn't respond. I'm hearing currently, however, that she's managing to make quite a name for herself. My sources tell me that she's the new star pupil of Winnie Katz's lesbian dance class.

RESCUE RANCH UPDATE

In March of this year the Utopia Rescue Ranch moved to a beautiful new home at Echo Hill. Cousin Nancy and her husband, Tony, continue to run the ranch, which fifty-seven dogs, four pigs, two cats, two donkeys, and one rooster currently call home. Nancy and Tony chose to keep the name Utopia, and given the spacious new surroundings, it seems all the more fitting. They also chose to keep their eighty-foot-long trailer which was moved almost fifty rugged miles in the dead of the night from Utopia to Echo Hill. The trailer made the arduous journey carrying only one passenger who steadfastly refused to leave its familiar confines. Lucky.

Special thanks are due to Laura Bush for her gracious support of our work at the Rescue Ranch. Her generosity of spirit inspires us all.

If you'd like to help out with a donation, adopt a dog, or just say hello, Cousin Nancy and Tony will be very happy to hear from you.

Utopia Rescue Ranch
966 Echo Hill Road
Medina, Texas 78055
tel: 830.589.7544
www.utopiarescue.com